Praise for Brendan O'Carrol
bestselling novel *The Ma*

"Cheerful . . . as unpretentious and
home-cooked meal . . . with a delicio
ending."—*The New York Times B*

"Reads like Frank McCourt's *Angela's Ashes* on
Prozac . . . Jaunty, charming."
—*Entertainment Weekly*

"How to lose weight: Read *The Mammy*. You will laugh your arse off and your tears will do away with your water-retention problem. It is an uproariously funny account of growing up in inner-city Dublin—a laugh-out-loud book with a Dickensian twist to it."
—Malachy McCourt, author of *A Monk Swimming*

The youngest of eleven children, BRENDAN O'CARROLL was born in North Dublin in 1955. An acclaimed playright and stand-up comedian, he is the creator of the popular Irish radio show, *Mrs Browne's Boys*. *The Mammy*, the first novel in his bestselling Mrs. Browne trilogy, was the basis for the feature film *Agnes Browne*, directed by and starring Anjelica Huston. *The Chisellers* and *The Granny* are the second and final books in the trilogy. All three novels are available in Plume editions.

"*The Mammy* is a heartwarming and very funny book." —Roddy Doyle, author of *Paddy Clarke Ha Ha Ha* and *A Star Called Henry*

"Irreverently comical."
—*Entertainment Weekly*

"O'Carroll has done one hell of a job capturing the absolute essence of a widowed mother of seven in working-class Dublin."
—Anjelica Huston

"Shades of O'Casey, as well as Brendan Behan. A story as colorful as Moore Street itself, but there is also pathos, compassion, and irony."
—*Entertainer*

"Hilarious and irreverent. A must-read."
—Gabriel Byrne

"These Dubliners are irresistibly charming . . . Tales of working-class Irish life now fill bookshelves, but there's space aplenty for O'Carroll's sturdy contribution."
—*Publishers Weekly*

"*The Mammy* is one of those books which almost demands to be read in one sitting, and its colorful descriptions of life in Dublin in the sixties will have Dublin natives feeling nostalgic and others feeling as if they were natives . . . *The Mammy* is guaranteed to make readers laugh. I didn't want to let go of Agnes Browne."
—*Irish Voice*

THE CHISELLERS

Brendan O'Carroll

A PLUME BOOK

PLUME
Published by Penguin Group
Penguin Group (USA) Inc., 375 Hudson Street, New York, New York 10014, U.S.A.
Penguin Group (Canada), 90 Eglinton Avenue East, Suite 700, Toronto, Ontario, Canada M4P 2Y3 (a division of Pearson Penguin Canada Inc.)
Penguin Books Ltd., 80 Strand, London WC2R 0RL, England
Penguin Ireland, 25 St. Stephen's Green, Dublin 2, Ireland
(a division of Penguin Books Ltd.)
Penguin Group (Australia), 250 Camberwell Road, Camberwell, Victoria 3124, Australia
(a division of Pearson Australia Group Pty. Ltd.)
Penguin Books India Pvt. Ltd., 11 Community Centre, Panchsheel Park,
New Delhi – 110 017, India
Penguin Books (NZ), 67 Apollo Drive, Rosedale, North Shore 0632, New Zealand
(a division of Pearson New Zealand Ltd.)
Penguin Group (South Africa) (Pty.) Ltd., 24 Sturdee Avenue, Rosebank,
Johannesburg 2196, South Africa

Penguin Books Ltd., Registered Offices: 80 Strand, London WC2R 0RL, England

First published by Plume, a member of Penguin Group (USA) Inc. Originally published in Ireland by The O'Brien Press.

First American Printing, March 2000

30 29 28 27 26 25 24 23 22 21

LIBRARY OF CONGRESS CATALOGING-IN-PUBLICATION DATA
O'Carroll, Brendan.
The chisellers / Brendan O'Carroll.
p. cm.
ISBN 978-0-452-28122-6
1. City and town life—Ireland—Dublin—Fiction. 2. Mother and child—Ireland—Dublin—Fiction. 3. Gangsters—Ireland—Dublin—Fiction. 4. Family—Ireland—Dublin—Fiction. 5. Dublin (Ireland)—Fiction. I. Title.
PR6065.C36 C48 2000
823'.914 21—dc21 99-046096

Printed in the United States of America

Introduction

Firstly let me thank you for buying this, my second novel. The success of my first offering *The Mammy*, published in 1994, took me completely by surprise. For this I thank all of you, readers, booksellers and my publishers.

The biggest thrill I have had from the fallout of *The Mammy*, has been the enormous number of people that have told me that it was the first book they had ever read. If you are one of those, I hope this is your second, that you have discovered the joy that books can bring and go on to entertain yourself with the thousands of wonderful, adventurous, mysterious, scary, and comical books that are lying on the shelves of bookstores right now whispering to all who pass them, 'Pick me ... Pick me!!'

I was introduced to the beauty of reading when I was just nine years old. A young schoolteacher named Billy Flood gave me a tattered copy of *Treasure Island*. Both that man and that book changed my life forever. Nothing, (O.K., with the possible exception of sex!) gives me more pleasure than a good book.

Writing a book is a very lonely task, and yet you do not really write alone, for without my partner and friend Gerry Browne spurring me on, or Evelyn, my secretary, checking over my nightly output (I do all my writing between midnight and 4am) or Tommy Swarbrigg taking the pressure off me just at the right time, or my co-workers in The Outrageous Comedy Show – Gerry Simpson, Shay, John, Bugsy, David Molloy and David Lang – making the extra time for me by doubling their efforts while we are on the road, without all of these, there would be no book. You will not see their names on the cover of this book, but take my word for it, their contribution was enormous, as it is in every venture we undertake. I am blessed to be playing with a great team.

Writers also need inspiration. Different things inspire different people. I am always inspired by people who succeed against the odds or who refuse to give up even when they are flat on their backs, and then rise to success with only their self-belief and courage as tools. These you will find remain humble people, finding no need to wear the badge of achievement on their sleeves, just content with the results of their endeavours in their hearts. Here are just some of the people who inspire me – some of the names you will recognise, some you won't: Gerry Browne, John Courtenay, Eamon Coghlan, Moya Doherty, Niall Quinn, Betty Hussey, Eileen Frei, Mary Cullen, Annie Browne, Eamon Gregg, Patricia Hoffman, John Fallon, Stephen Collins, Roddy Doyle, Nell McCafferty, Brendan Daly and, of course, Doreen O'Carroll. Every one of them a hero!

Brendan O'Carroll
DUBLIN 1995

Now she stands alone, pregnant and deserted,
What she thought was love has left her broken hearted,
Who are we to say, true love has what meaning?
In a young girl's mind, life can be so simple ...

From the song
'Sixteen Years of Age'
by Gerry Browne.

This book I dedicate with all my heart to

Dolly Dowdall

a good mother-in-law for eighteen years

and a welcome friend for twenty-seven years.

Prologue

LONDON 1970

MANNY WISE READ OVER THE SHORT DOCUMENT once again. He smiled. His weekend visit back to his father's home in Ireland had not been a waste of time. His father's business itself was not doing well. But the property the factory was on was located in Dublin's city centre and without doubt would be of value when the old man kicked the bucket. Everything had worked out very well. He had only intended his short visit to yield him a few pounds from the old man. He needed only two grand to put together this Amsterdam deal that would establish him as one of the major players in the cocaine business in London.

Thankfully he arrived to find the old man very sick and bed-ridden. His doctor had him drugged up to the eyeballs. Manny got his money – and getting his father to sign the document that transferred everything he owned over to his son Manny 'For love and natural affection' had been easy, the man was so confused.

Manny read the legal phrase again, 'For love and natural affection'. He laughed aloud, though nobody heard him as he was alone in the study of his five-roomed apartment on Edgeware Road WC1. What was laughable about the phrase was that there was not one shred of love between the two men.

Manny folded the document and inserted it into an envelope on which he wrote 'Dublin Papers', then placed it in the safe below his bookcase, alongside the £10,000 cash that was ready for the Amsterdam people. It would be there for him when the time came, sooner he hoped rather than later. As he closed the door and spun the combination dial he said aloud, 'Thanks, Pop! You fucking loser.'

PART I

Chapter 1

DUBLIN 1970

AS HE SAT ON HIS HIGH STOOL behind the podium, centre-stage, Pat Muldoon scanned the assembly before him. It was an impressive sight. An audience of five hundred at least, all sitting facing him with their heads bowed. The silence was eerie, the only sound in this packed room being the whirring of the bingo machine as it tossed its numbered balls and fed them up the tube at random. Pat Muldoon had been calling the bingo numbers in St Francis Xavier Hall since 1962. In those eight years never before had he seen the 'Snowball' reach the massive sum that it stood at tonight. The makeshift sign outside the hall announced the record amount: 'Snowball now standing at £615 and 53 calls!' He knew it would be won tonight. The first person to shout CHECK before he extracted the fifty-third number would take it all! He read the number on the ball in his hand and called, 'All the fours – forty-four!'

The bingo nights at the Francis Xavier Hall each Wednesday and Friday would usually attract an average of two hundred and fifty to three hundred people. It was the size of the Snowball which had doubled the crowd in the last three weeks. Extra chairs were borrowed from the

Community Centre to accommodate the influx of strangers that arrived from every corner of Dublin. Still, the regulars who sat on the same chairs every Wednesday and every Friday, week-in week-out, were not discommoded in any way – that was important for they were the ones who would be there when the Snowball went back down to just one hundred pounds.

About two-thirds of the way down the hall, and close to the toilets, sat Agnes Browne and her merry group of six. Next to Agnes was Carmel Dowdall, a neighbour of Agnes's in James Larkin Court. Like Agnes, Carmel had a thirteen-year-old daughter. Coincidentally, both young girls were named Cathy, and they were best pals both in and out of school. Sitting beside Carmel was a large red-faced woman, built like a man and adding to this by wearing her husband's crombie coat. This was Nelly Robinson. A long-time friend of Agnes's, Nelly was a dealer in Moore Street with a stall no more than fifty feet from Agnes's own pitch. Sitting facing these three were Nelly's twin daughters, affectionately known to all the dealers in the market as Splish and Splash. The twin girls had matured well, and although quite pretty, at nineteen had still not managed to secure themselves either husbands or steady boyfriends – probably because, thanks to a lisp they shared, they had an inability to say 'Give us a kiss' without covering their suitor in spittle. The last of the six was an elderly man. This was Bunnie Morrissey. Agnes and the other women knew Bunnie only from the bingo nights. A long-time widower, Bunnie, like many others, used the bingo as a reason to get out for the night. He would arrive every Wednesday and Friday with a plastic check multi-coloured shopping bag, from which he would remove his bingo board and clip, his two bingo pens – one red, one black – and, last of all, a single tattered tartan carpet slipper.

This last item had an interesting history. Two years previously, while coming down the stairs of his tiny pensioner's flat in Dorset Street, Bunnie slipped and twisted his ankle. The subsequent swelling meant that Bunnie could not get his right shoe onto his foot. So that evening Bunnie had arrived at the bingo wearing just one shoe, on his left foot, and on his swollen right foot this carpet slipper. After fifteen years of bingo-playing, that night was the first time that Bunnie ever won anything – he collected £15 for a full house, and for the couple of seconds it took him to call 'Check', he was the focus of every eye in the hall. Since then Bunnie never started a night of bingo without first slipping off his right shoe and putting on his tatty 'lucky' carpet slipper. Sadly, since that night Bunnie had failed to win a single penny, and each session would end with him firing the slipper into the plastic bag, grunting, 'Lucky slipper, me bollix!' Yet, before every game every night of the bingo, out would come the lucky slipper again.

'One and seven – seventeen.' Mr Muldoon called out the twelfth number.

Suddenly a cry of 'Check' went up and all heads lifted simultaneously and looked in the direction of the hand in the air holding the salmon-coloured bingo book and claiming the line prize.

'Only twelve calls? That's early,' mused Agnes aloud.

'Yeah, it is, very early,' replied Nelly, as the two stared over at the upraised hand.

'Who is it?' asked Carmel.

'Yer woman with the yellow teeth from Sheriff Street, Clarke I think her name is. Her husband does the telegrams, rides a motor bike,' Agnes informed the group.

'I hear that's not all he rides,' remarked Nelly, and they all burst into laughter.

The burst of laughter brought a look from the line winner, Mrs Clarke. Agnes caught her gaze and waved to her with a smile. 'Have it and you'll get it!' she shouted. The woman smiled and waved back.

Bunnie was too bothered to laugh with the others. 'I hardly have a fuckin' mark at all!' he grumbled.

The twins, too, were preoccupied.

'Ma, did he call tirty sisks?' asked Splish, spraying Agnes's knees.

'No, not yet. I don't think so.'

'Bunnie, d'you know, did he call tirty sisks?' Splish tried again.

'What are yeh askin' me for?' snapped Bunnie, still annoyed about his bad luck. 'Sure I hardly have a fuckin' mark at all.' He spoke as if Splish were to blame for his lack of marks.

There now followed a short interval during which the claim for a line would be checked. With only twelve numbers gone it was looking very likely that the Snowball would indeed be won this evening. Agnes used the interval opportunity to light up a cigarette, as did most of the other bingo players. The room was a-buzz with anticipation as everyone realised the early call on a line meant that most probably the Snowball would go.

Agnes blew out the match and exhaled the first drag, then, picking a piece of tobacco off her tongue, she turned to Carmel.

'You know,' she announced suddenly, 'your Cathy's language has gone to the dogs.'

'Wha', Agnes?' Carmel asked, not catching Agnes's drift.

'Your Cathy – her language has gone to the dogs.'

Carmel thought for a moment, then began to nod her head. 'D'yeh know, Agnes you're right. It's fuckin' dreadful. And she's an imperint little bitch as well. I think she gets the bad language off the O'Briens in eighty-one, fuckers they are.'

The bingo ball machine began to whirl again and as the audience prepared themselves, Mr Muldoon called. 'Here we go for the full house, and the Snowball. Eyes down and your first number is ... '

Every pen in the hall hovered and the electricity of anticipation was so strong you could almost hear it hum.

'Two fat ladies – eighty-eight.'

After a further eight numbers, Agnes was able to mark off seven. Nelly, noticing the constant moving of Agnes's pen half-whispered to her, 'Jaysus, Agnes, you're flyin'.'

'I know. Shut up, you'll put the mockers on me!'

'It's well for yeh. I haven't a fuckin' mark at all,' piped in Bunnie.

'Shush,' said Agnes as Mr Muldoon called out the next number.

'Was she worth it? Two and six – twenty-six.'

Agnes didn't have twenty-six – and she didn't have the next six numbers either. But over the next fifteen calls she steadily marked off a couple of twos and threes called in a row, until she suddenly realised her card was starting to fill up, and with just four calls to go she had only one number left. The number seven.

'Jaysus – I have a wait!' Agnes said to nobody in particular.

'Agnes has a wait,' echoed Carmel, passing on the news.

'Oh Mammy, me nerves!' mumbled Splish, picking up the sudden tension.

'Come on – number seven,' said Agnes fervently, as if she were in prayer.

'Two little ducks – twenty-two.'

'Number seven, number seven – come on, number seven,' Agnes was intoning now.

'Pull it, mister ... Pull it! ... Oh Jaysus, Agnes.' This was Carmel.

'Shut up, shut up! Come on, number seven.'

'There's only two calls to go,' says Bunnie, 'and I'm still waiting on three more numbers. I'm out of the runnin'.'

'Top of the house – ninety.'

Agnes held her hand up to her now-perspiring forehead. 'Ah what's wrong with yeh, mister! Come on, number seven.'

'And this is the final call for the Snowball ...'

'On its own, number seven, please God. On its own, number seven,' Agnes groaned.

'On its own ...'

'Yes! Yes! Call it – seven!

'– number four.'

There was momentary silence and a collective intake of breath in the hall as everybody waited for the inevitable call of 'Check'. But it didn't come. Hardly anybody except those in her company heard Agnes's groan. The non-event was met with a mixture of sighs, moans and then giggles in the knowledge that the big Snowball would be there yet again this coming Friday – only even bigger, and with the calls moving up to fifty-four, it had to be won!

Mr Muldoon moved on, wondering at the back of his mind where he was going to get the extra chairs he would need for Friday's session.

'Unlucky for some – thirteen.'

Still no call. Although the Snowball was now gone, the full house would still be worth fifty pounds. Not to be sneezed at, not to be sneezed at at all.

'One little duck – number two.'

Bunnie Morrissey's attempt to jump straight up was thwarted. The pushing of his full weight onto the back of the chair in his effort to spring up split the cross member of the chair and as it splintered and collapsed he fell backwards. His right leg shot up like the blade of a flick-knife, sending his lucky slipper flying across the room, where it caught an elderly woman full in the face, mashing her Woodbine against her heavily lipsticked mouth and sending sparks in all directions. As the back of Bunnie's head hit the ground a barely audible gurgle of 'Check' came from him.

Mr Muldoon, not realising what was happening and thinking there was just a slight commotion, exclaimed, 'Keep it quiet there, please.'

To which Bunnie, now spread-eagled on his back, his bingo pen lying ten feet from him and his right arm stretched upright, perpendicular to his body and clasping the bingo board, screamed, 'Check! For fuck's sake, check.'

'We have a check down the middle of the hall.'

Agnes looked over at Bunnie and stood up. For a moment Bunnie thought she was going to give him a hand up, but instead she put her hands on her hips and exclaimed, 'Bunnie Morrissey, yeh auld bollix!'

* * *

In the three years since the untimely death of Redser Browne, his widow Agnes and her seven children had flourished. Mark, the eldest boy, continued his training as a carpenter. Frankie was a handsome sixteen-year-old, though it was difficult to see it sometimes, for he'd had his head completely shaved, wore a tartan shirt and wide parallel denims which were cut between the knee and the ankle to reveal tartan socks over which he wore a pair of blood-red Doc Marten bovver boots. This was the fashion for 'skinheads'. The fad had begun in Britain with groups of white youths who spent their evenings drinking cider, dancing to reggae music, and then, like packs of wolves, would hunt down and beat Pakistanis, Indians, West Indians, and homosexuals of any creed or colour. Frankie and the gang of thugs he hung out with were starved for targets. Dublin did not have a population of Indians, West Indians or coloureds in general, so the homosexuals took the full brunt. Failing an encounter with a homosexual, these gangs would use anyone that looked weak – at least weaker than they were. He didn't even realise it himself, but Frankie Browne was a neo-Nazi.

This posed some problems for his younger brother Rory. As soon as he reached the working age of fourteen, Rory quit school, and was now one year into a hairdressing apprenticeship. Monday after Monday, Rory would see his working colleagues and friends bruised and scarred from the weekend attacks by skinhead gangs – to a skinhead, all male hairdressers were 'queers'. Rory kept his mind on his work, which he loved, and trod home carefully each evening. Rory spoke little to Frankie and trusted him less.

Dermot Browne, on the other hand, was everybody's friend – bursting with energy, full of laughter and always up to some mischief or other. His golden hair would glisten in the sunlight as he dashed about the football field displaying his talents. He was popular too with the girls. His fair skin and smiling blue eyes made him the heart throb of most of his sister Cathy's friends.

Unfortunately, such was not the case with Dermot's twin brother Simon. Although he stammered less as he got older, the cast in his left eye was still there and still obvious. This gained him the nickname 'Giddy Eye'. Like Dermot, Simon was in his first year at St Declan's Technical School. But unlike Dermot, who seemed to excel at everything he touched, Simon had yet to find his particular talent in life. It was not carpentry. He seemed to have an inability to draw a straight line, and on one occasion nearly sawed off his left arm. It was not metalwork. He was no longer allowed to use the welding torch in class after welding a piece of angle-iron to the vice. The one thing he was good at was religious knowledge. He loved praying, and felt secure in the silence of the church, where he would sit for hours alone. His religious knowledge teacher thought that he might even have a vocation. Another of his talents was finding things. Agnes would call Simon her little St Anthony, and whenever anything was lost or misplaced Agnes would simply say, 'Wait till Simon comes home, he'll find it.' Right enough, within minutes of coming home Simon would find the errant object.

Cathy Browne, at thirteen years of age, was in sixth class, her final year, in the Mother of Divine Providence Girls' School. Since her battle with Sister Mary Magdalen three years previously, Cathy was more or less left alone, and began to flourish in school, so much so that she now had thoughts of going on to secondary school, something never before achieved by any Browne.

Trevor, at six, was doing a second year at first class. He had also had two years of 'high babies'. Trevor was called 'a slow child', a term Agnes didn't really understand. Trevor's teacher, Miss Thomas, once asked Agnes if there was any history of dyslexia in the family, and Agnes, thinking it was some kind of tropical disease, emphatically answered No – 'Sure they've never been out of the country.'

Agnes herself looked really well. Things had got a lot better in the last couple of years, with both Mark and Rory now bringing in a wage. Every week Rory handed up £2 and Mark £9, which was all but £1/15/– of his wages. The black-and-white television which Mark had rented back in 1967 had now been replaced by a colour set. The sitting-room and both bedrooms of the flat had carpets, and even though the kitchen still had linoleum, it was good flexible linoleum, not the kind that cracked when you bent it. And now that she could afford it, Agnes had her hair done once a month. She went to Wash & Blow, the salon where Rory was training, where she received a 20 percent discount thanks to Rory. It's amazing what a hairdo can do to lift a woman's spirits.

That's just what Agnes was thinking as she ran the brush slowly through her raven-black hair. She smiled at herself in the mirror. She was thinking of Bunnie Morrissey and how funny it had been the night before seeing him lying on his back screaming 'Check'. She giggled to herself. Outside in the hall she heard the letterbox clatter and the 'pflap' of the post as it landed on the doormat. She placed the hairbrush down on her dressing-table, went out to the hall and picked up the mail. She tucked it under her arm, went to the steaming kettle and made herself a mug of tea. She carried the mug to the kitchen table, lit up a cigarette and began to open the letters.

There were three letters in the post this morning. The light blue envelope edged in red and navy stripes and with the Canadian stamp on it was easily recognisable as a letter from Agnes's sister Dolly. No, not Dolly now, now it's Dolores, Mrs Dolores Gowland. Agnes smiled to herself. Dolly had emigrated to Toronto fifteen years previously in 1955, and for the first two or three years signed all her letters 'Dolly'. In 1957 she began to go out with Larry Gowland, who worked 'in a bank, no less', and after a courtship of three years she had married the poor chap. So it was, from 1960 onwards, Dolly Redden signed all her letters Dolores Gowland.

Once Agnes had opened the envelope and unfolded the letter, the two crisp $20 bills that always accompanied one of Dolly's letters fell to the table. 'God bless yeh, Dolly,' Agnes said aloud. The letter was full of the usual news about how Dolly's two children, Jason and Melissa, were doing at school and the latest news of Larry's upward climb in the bank. Agnes wondered what ailment Dolly had this month – Dolly was a hypochondriac. It came in the third paragraph: dermatitis. Agnes read the word and said it a couple of times to herself, 'Dermatitis, der-ma-ti-tis.' She looked up from the letter at Mark and Dermot who were sitting sideways on the couch facing each other.

'Mark!' she called.

'Yes, Ma.'

'What's dermatitis?'

Instead it was Dermot who answered. 'It's a thing that foreigners do get 'cause they don't wipe their arse proper.' Both Mark and Dermot howled with laughter.

Agnes said, 'Don't be so disgusting you, yeh brat,' but she smiled too.

'It is, I swear,' said Dermot, who would swear to anything at the drop of a hat.

'Is it, Mark?' asked Agnes.

Mark shook his head, still chuckling. 'Honestly, Ma, I don't know.'

Agnes went back to her letter, a frown now creasing her forehead as she wondered what kind of filthy habits her sister had picked up since she had emigrated to Canada.

The reason Mark and Dermot were sitting on the couch facing each other was because of the 'test'. The test was Mark's final exam in technical college. Now seventeen, Mark had spent his last three years attending carpentry college on a part-time basis, while still doing his apprenticeship with Wise & Co., Furniture Manufacturers since 1940. Since joining Wise's over two and a half years ago, Mark had worked hard and applied himself to the trade. He loved his job. He whistled on his way to work each morning, and devoted himself to each task Mr Wise set him. As he worked on bentwood backs for chairs or claw-and-ball legs, his enthusiasm was that of the dedicated artist to his piece. Indeed, some of the work he turned out, even with just two and a half years' training, had Mr Wise glowing with pride in his young prodigy. Though Mark still had a year and a half of practical work to go through before he qualified, Mr Wise told Agnes on many occasions that Mark was as good as some of the fully trained men who were a long time in the business, and bigger and stronger than most. At only seventeen years of age, Mark was already a half-inch over six feet and as he started to fill out, he definitely had the potential of being a young bullock.

Young Dermot, on the other hand, had got his growth hormones from Agnes's side of the family. Compared with other boys of fourteen years of age, Dermot was slight and short. When describing him to strangers, Agnes would say, 'There wouldn't be enough elastic in his underpants to make a pair of garters for a budgie.' Having said that, she would also add that whatever he might lack in physical stature, he well made up for in sheer cunning, ingenuity and inventiveness. For Dermot Browne was so streetwise one would think he had invented the term.

For a moment Agnes stared at the two boys. There was a bond between them that ignored the thirty-one months' age difference. She saw it in Dermot's eyes – they sparkled in admiration as he listened to every word uttered by his older brother, as if each one were a never-to-be-forgotten gem of wisdom. She saw it in the beam of Mark's smile each time Dermot entered the room, and she felt it in the shared laughter as they each recalled the day's happenings, Mark in Wise's and Dermot in St Declan's Technical School for Boys. The tales were elongated and exaggerated, but that didn't matter because the fun was in the telling and not in the truth.

Turning her attention back to the post, Agnes first folded the two $20 bills and tucked them carefully away in her purse. She would exchange them later that day in the post office for £32. The second letter Agnes opened was from Mr Cartwright, the principal of St Declan's Technical School, where Frankie, Dermot and Simon were pupils. The letter was about Frankie and his attendance – or lack of it. Mr Cartwright indicated that he was now at the end of his tether with Frankie, and he suggested that Agnes pay him a visit as soon as possible to discuss the boy. Agnes rested her head on her hand and sighed deeply. She just couldn't understand what was wrong with Frankie. Of all her six boys she was easiest on him. Yet he never seemed to be happy. Time and time again Agnes gave in to Frankie's rebellious ways. Yet the easier she was on him it seemed, the worse he became. There was great friction between Mark and Frankie, although the boys, particularly Mark, went to great lengths to avoid any displays of open hostility in front of Agnes. Frankie came and went as he wished, and Mark rarely spoke to him or about him.

Mark looked up from his instruction manual and saw the jaded look on Agnes's face. 'What is it, Ma?'

'Frankie's been missin' school again,' she replied, her heart heavy.

'Again?'

'Yes, luv – again.'

Dermot got up and quietly left the room, mumbling that he was heading for the toilet. He had no urge nor need to go to the toilet, but had a sneaking feeling that if he remained in the room he would be called upon as a witness. Brownes don't snitch.

Mark closed the book and slowly walked over to the kitchen table and sat facing his mother.

'Ma, I don't want to snitch, but you must know he

spends his bleedin' time hangin' around with those scumbag friends of his, roamin' around the streets all day in and out of bookie's shops.'

'Bookie's! Sure where would he get the money?' asked Agnes.

Mark looked away from her. 'You tell me, Ma.'

They both knew where he got the money. Most mornings Agnes's purse would be a little bit lighter than the night before. With seven children, it was hard to accuse one – all children are a little light-fingered – but in her heart Agnes knew that the odd half-crown or two shillings that vanished each day was going into Frankie's pocket. She didn't dare accuse Frankie openly or even voice her suspicion, for she knew full well that Mark would set upon him and she recalled from her own childhood days that nothing was more vicious than family fights.

'D'yeh want me to talk to him?' asked Mark, knowing the answer before Agnes's reply.

'No. God no. I'll speak to him myself,' she replied quickly – too quickly.

'Well, yeh'd better, Ma, 'cause I've just about had enough of him! I don't mind handin' up me money, but it's for the flat, and the younger ones, not for the bookie's, or cider.'

Mark rose as he said this and went back to the couch where he picked up his instruction manual and began to study again.

It was a direct accusation, but Agnes let it go. She really couldn't defend Frankie. Agnes made a mental note to call up the next day to St Declan's and speak to the principal. She folded the letter and put it into her apron pocket and turned her attention to the final letter that had arrived that morning.

This one had a crest on the envelope: the three castles of Dublin. She knew it came from the Corporation, though she was a little bit puzzled. The only time she received a letter from Dublin Corporation was when her rent was in arrears. But she was up-to-date now and had been for the last year. She ripped open the flap and extracted a very official-looking letter. It read:

Dear Tenant,

Dublin Corporation is pleased to announce the implementation of its Inner City Renewal Plan. The long-term plan is to eradicate the inner city tenement situation.

The plan will be implemented over the next five years and will be carried out on a zone-by-zone basis. (A map of the zones is available at the Dublin Corporation Housing Offices for viewing.)

The area encompassing Lower Gardiner Street, Sean McDermott Street West, St Jarlath's Street, James Larkin Court and James Larkin Road is Zone One.

Demolition on this zone will begin July 1970. Residents will be re-housed in new ultra-modern suburban housing estates to be built in Cabra, Dublin 7; Finglas, Dublin 11; and Coolock, Dublin 5. Houses and areas have been drawn for families on a lottery basis and you have drawn:

43, Wolfe Tone Grove,
Finglas West,
Dublin 11.

All homes are two-storey dwellings with three bedrooms, one reception room, bathroom, toilet and kitchen, front and back gardens.

On behalf of the city manager and Dublin County Council, I wish you good fortune in your new home.

Yours sincerely,

James Jackson
Housing Officer
Dublin Corporation

'Mother of Jesus!' Agnes exclaimed.
'What?' Mark asked.
'We're bein' turfed out.'
'Turfed out? What d'yeh mean, turfed out?'
Shocked, Agnes looked at Mark. 'They're knockin' down the buildin's – and they're sendin' us down the country!'

Chapter 2

WHEN THE ALARM CLOCK BLARED at 4am the next morning Agnes stretched her arm out, and felt around on her bedside locker before landing on the clock to switch it off. She couldn't open her eyes, the lids felt like they were glued together. She had had just three hours' sleep, having waited up for Frankie until one o'clock to try and talk to him. He hadn't arrived by then, so she went to bed.

Slowly she rose and reset the alarm for 6.30. On her way to the bathroom she tiptoed into the boys' room and gently placed the ticking clock beside Mark. The boys now all had a mattress each, thanks to Mark. He had bought some planed deal and webbing from Mr Wise at wholesale prices, and the boys' room now had six built-in bunks, three against each wall. All six boys were asleep. Agnes had to stretch up a little to look into Frankie's bunk. He was there sleeping, and her nose tingled at the smell of stale cider. He was also fully clothed. She bit her bottom lip and closed her eyes, and then she sighed deeply and left the room, shutting the door gently behind her.

Agnes got stuck into her usual morning chores. She began by making the six packed lunches. Then, into the bathroom where she rinsed and wrung out the wash she had left soaking in the bath the night before. Then she hung all the washing on the clothes line out the back window. She wedged a pole between the line and the windowsill to make a triangular line. The only thing she had washed that did not go on the line was the beautiful pink cashmere jumper that Pierre had bought her the previous Christmas. For this she laid a towel flat on the ground, placed the jumper on top of the towel and then laid another towel on top of the jumper. She gathered up three pairs of trousers, one belonging to Dermot, one belonging to Rory and one belonging to Mark, along with her own gabardine coat; she would leave them into Marlowe's cleaners in O'Connell Street later. By 4.30am she was sitting having a cup of tea and a cigarette. Ten minutes later it was down the stairs, out with the pram and the two bread-boards and she headed out into the still-dark morning for her twenty-minute walk to the fruit markets. One and three quarter hours later Agnes was in Moore Street throwing up the canvas roof over her stall, while back in 92 James Larkin Court the alarm clock burst into life at Mark's pillow.

Mark switched it off and rose quickly, pulled on a pair of denim jeans, zipped up the fly and went to the kitchen. At the cooker he turned on all four gas rings – there was a little 'putt, putt' as each ring burst into life. He would leave them burning while he washed himself and brushed his teeth, and this would take the chill off the kitchen. He went to the bathroom and washed. On his way back to the bedroom he turned off the gas rings. The kitchen was nice and cosy. He then went to the bedroom and gently woke Dermot.

'Dermo, Dermo – the papers, Dermo.' He spoke in a hushed tone.

Groggily Dermot muttered, 'What?'

'The papers. It's twenty to seven. Come on, yeh'll be late.'

Since Mark had joined Wise's, Dermot had taken over his paper round. Dermot was not as willing a worker as Mark and found it really difficult each morning to whip up the enthusiasm for running around in the cold and rain, shoving newspapers through letterboxes.

By the time Dermot had washed and dressed, Mark had a mug of tea ready for each of them, and some toast dripping in butter. They both tucked in.

'What happened last night with Frankie?' Dermot asked, wiping butter from his chin.

'I don't know,' Mark said, off-hand.

'Did she kill him?'

'I don't think so. I didn't hear anythin' anyway.'

'The school are going to expel him. I heard the master sayin' it yesterday.'

'I don't blame them. He's a wanker.'

'He's not, he's just ... different,' Dermot defended Frankie.

'Ah, you're too young to understand.'

'What d'yeh mean? I'm only two and a half years younger than you.'

'Yeh, well, two and a half years is a long time. When you were born I was already walkin', pal.' Mark emphasised his words by pointing a crust of toast at Dermot.

Dermot looked at him for a moment and then very seriously said, 'Are yeh walkin' since you were two and a half?'

'Yep,' Mark answered.

'Jaysus, yeh must be knackered.'

The two boys howled with laughter and Mark dropped the crust onto the plate, picked up his cup and walked to the sink where he left the cup on the draining board.

'Right, let's go,' he announced.

He tossed Dermot his duffel coat and put on his own donkey jacket and the two boys headed off to work.

* * *

Agnes took her break at 10am, leaving Fat Annie to mind the stall. It took her just five minutes to walk to Dublin Corporation's Housing Section in Jervis Street. She was not prepared for the sight that met her when she arrived there. It was absolute bedlam. It seemed that every resident in Zone One had arrived simultaneously to protest. The hallways were chock-a-block with people, all chattering and grumbling. Halfway down the hall, standing beside a bench, was a tall man with silver-grey hair, in a suit, shirt and tie, and wearing bifocals. Most of the complaints and abuse seemed to be aimed at him.

Agnes recognised Birdie Kerrigan from St Jarlath's Street. The Kerrigans had lived in Dublin's inner city for nigh on a hundred years. Birdie looked frightened and confused.

'Mornin', Birdie. This is bloody awful,' Agnes said to her.

'Coolock, Agnes! Fuckin' Coolock! Where the fuck is Coolock, Agnes?' she exclaimed tearfully.

'I know, luv, it's dreadful,' Agnes tried to console her.

But Birdie went on, 'The kids will never find their way home! I can't even fuckin' spell Coolock!' Birdie was distraught.

Agnes linked Birdie's arm and patted her on the

shoulder, knowing that Birdie couldn't even spell 'town'. But, no matter, she understood what Birdie meant. There must have been a hundred people there just like Birdie, panicking and worrying about their future. To the officials in the Corporation it was just relocation, but to these people who had been part of Dublin's inner city all of their lives it was akin to deportation. Eventually the silver-haired man in the bifocals stood up on the bench and started stamping his heel. Then raising his arms in the air he cried, 'Silence please! Will everybody please calm down.'

Gradually the halls quietened and all heads turned to the Corporation man. He had a County Meath accent.

'Ladies and gentlemen, my name is Benny Lynch. I am a placement officer in the housing executive.'

'Fuck you and the housin' executive – we're not movin',' a voice called from the middle of the crowd.

This was met with a huge cheer. Again the silver-haired official raised his hands in the air. He was now perspiring, and he wanted to be anywhere but here. When he had silence again he went on.

'The homes that are being built for you are ultra-modern first-class dwellings,' he assured them.

'Good. Then you move to fuckin' Finglas and leave us alone,' a woman's voice cried.

Again a huge cheer.

The official didn't raise his arms this time, but still silence fell over the crowd. He spoke again.

'If you will try to be orderly I will take all of your names and register your protest. However, I have to tell you that the decision has been made. Dublin Corporation is set on progress in the city and the decision is irrevocable.'

A mumbling started around the crowd. He raised his voice slightly. 'But let me say this!' Dead silence came again. 'The areas you are being moved out of will be rebuilt with homes – new homes, better homes, more modern homes – and all of you will be entitled to apply to be relocated back in the inner city if you wish.'

This was a surprise announcement and seemed to calm everyone down a bit.

'How long will that take?' a man at the front of the crowd asked.

The silver-haired man answered with authority. 'We expect the houses in Zone One – your zone – to be ready for occupation in the summer of 1973.'

'That's three and a half years, for Christ's sake!' a woman cried out.

'I know,' the official shouted down to her. 'But this is a huge project and these things take time. Let's face it, you people cannot go on living the way you are at present. Now, these new homes in Cabra, Finglas and Coolock will have hot running water, gardens, three bedrooms!'

There were mumblings of, 'We'll live the way we want to live,' and 'good enough for our parents good enough for us'. But deep in their heart of hearts they all knew he was right, and still they held on to the vague promise that they would eventually be moved back into the city centre. The silver-haired man saw he was winning. He should have quit while he was ahead, but instead he went for one more victory blow. 'Ladies and gentlemen, progress is a huge machine. Me? I'm just a tool.'

'Yeh can say that again,' shouted a little old lady, and the hall burst into nervous laughter.

The man's face reddened and he vanished into an office. The crowd filed out onto the street and within a couple of minutes they had dispersed.

Like it or not, come July, Agnes Browne and family were moving to Finglas.

Chapter 3

SEAN MCHUGH WAS SIXTY-EIGHT YEARS OF AGE, his wife Poppy sixty-seven. He had two children, Michael and Sheila, and both had emigrated long ago. Michael was a truck driver in Boston, Massachusetts, and Sheila was a supervisor in a plastics factory in Maidenstone in London. Sean had married Poppy in a hurry in 1921 in John's Lane church, not because she was pregnant but because he thought for sure he was going to die. He fought on Michael Collins's side in the Civil War, and nobody was more relieved than he when it ended in 1922. Sean was sad to see so many young Irishmen die at the hands of other Irishmen, particularly his Commander-in-Chief Michael Collins, after whom Sean had named his son. Sean had joined the Free State Army for a short time, but after four years had had enough of it and in 1927 he went on the dole. He picked up some part-time jobs here and there over the next six years, but in 1933 he went to work as a general factory help for a middle-aged Jewish Austrian man who had just come to Ireland.

Benjamin Wisemann was thirty-three years of age when he landed in Dun Laoghaire in 1933 – he immediately shortened his name to Wise. It had been a long, tough journey, and his wife Anna had spent the three weeks that they'd travelled fussing over Manny, their son. Manny was just ten years old and treated Anna like a servant rather than his mother. Benjamin disliked the boy and was often dismayed that as a father he should feel this way about his son. But Manny just took and took and took, and Anna gave and gave until she had no more to give. In September 1944, two weeks before Manny's twenty-first birthday, Anna passed away. Manny had been living in England for just under a year at that stage. He did not come home for the funeral. Manny was a schmuck.

Sean McHugh remembered the boy and the efforts his father made to bring him into the trade, but Manny simply had no interest. It was not just that he had no interest in the furniture business, he had no interest in anything that involved work.

Mr Wise was passionate about woodworking. He had such a depth of knowledge about it. This knowledge and training he gladly passed on to Sean McHugh, and Sean was a willing pupil. Sean McHugh rose to be Mr Benny Wise's right-hand man. Mr Wise would go away for weeks at a time, selling furniture all over England, in the full knowledge that as long as Sean was there everything would be safe back in Ireland. He was right, for Sean had Wise & Co. running like a well-oiled Swiss watch.

As Sean sat now in the foreman's office in Wise's he

wondered to himself where the twenty-seven years had gone since he first walked in that door. He was also worried. Over the last five years, business at Wise's had taken a nose-dive. Now Sean held in his hand a letter from Smyth & Blythe Distributors in England, Wise's biggest customer. Gregory Smyth stated that he would be in Dublin this coming Monday and he would like to sit down and have a serious talk with Mr Wise. Sean knew what that meant. He had over the last five years seen similar letters from Coppinger of Manchester, McDonald's of Glasgow and O'Neill's of Belfast. Smyth & Blythe were dropping their business with Wise's. This would leave Wise & Co. with only its Irish customers – Cavendishes, Sloan's, Arnott's and Brown Thomas in Dublin, Cash's in Cork and Shaw's in Limerick. Not enough, Sean knew, to keep Wise's open. Mr Wise blamed this new-fangled plywood- and chipboard-framed furniture.

'Nobody wants quality any more!' Mr Wise would say, exasperated, and Sean would just nod his head. 'Soon, Sean, I tell you for sure, there will be no carpenters – just assemblers.'

Sean had dropped into Mr Wise on his way to work that day. Poor old Benny was not well, not well at all. He told Sean he wouldn't be into work, so Sean didn't inform him about the letter from Smyth & Blythe. Sean would go and meet them himself. Mr Wise's ill-health was not helped by the fact that he knew that Wise's was going down the tubes. The factory, which once had forty staff, now had barely twenty, and twelve of those were apprentices. Mr Wise, Sean thought, would die with the business.

He placed the letter in the open ledger on his desk, looked at his watch and realised it was tea-break time.

He stood and walked towards the door to the factory, picking up his whistle on the way. He stepped just outside the door and blew the whistle three times very loudly. The machines began to wind down and within thirty seconds the factory was quiet as the workers filed into the canteen to make tea and eat their sandwiches. As he was about to step back into his office, he heard in the distance the tap, tap, tap of somebody still working, down at the far right-hand corner of the factory. He smiled to himself. He knew who it was. He headed off down the factory floor, picking up odd pieces of wood here and there and putting them in a bin, until he rounded the corner and, behind a pile of hardwood, saw the back of Mark Browne's head. He walked over to where the young man was working.

'Didn't yeh hear the whistle, Mark?' He spoke to the back of Mark's head.

Mark turned and smiled at him. 'I did, Mr McHugh. That's okay, I have me sandwiches here. I'll have them as I'm working. I'm not really a tea man, if yeh know what I mean.'

Sean dug his large hands into the pockets of his dungarees. 'Christ, Mark, if I had ten like you, I'd put this factory back on its feet!'

'Thanks, Mr McHugh.'

'That's okay, son. I really mean it.' Sean began to walk away, then stopped and turned back to the boy. He suddenly had a notion. 'Mark?'

Mark looked up. He had three pin-nails in his mouth but still managed to answer. 'Yes, Mr McHugh?'

'I'd like you to do something with me on Monday.'

Sean McHugh spent the next twenty minutes telling

Mark the situation at Wise's. Explaining who Smyth & Blythe were, and how important they were to the future of the business, Sean told Mark he felt that if somebody young went along to this meeting then Smyth & Blythe might regain a bit of confidence in Wise's, seeing some new blood. He didn't know if it would work, but it was worth a try. 'So what do you think, Mark, will you do it?'

'Well yeh, sure, Mr McHugh, if you think it will help. But I've never been to a meetin' before – what'll I wear?'

Sean laughed and patted the boy on the back. 'A shirt and tie will be fine, Mark.'

'A shirt and tie. Okay, then.'

Sean went back to his office a little lighter on his feet and for some reason that he couldn't explain to himself, his heart a little happier! Mark slowly placed three more nails in his mouth, stooped down to the roll-top desk he was working on and said aloud to himself, 'Where the fuck will I get a shirt and tie?'

* * *

Agnes sat ashen-faced across the table from the principal of St Declan's Technical School. She could not honestly defend Frankie. She wanted to think that this man was just a crabby old school principal who for some reason was picking on her son, but in her heart she knew this wasn't true. Frankie, she had to admit to herself, but only in her mind, was a bad egg.

'Frankly, Mrs Browne, we see the binman more often at the school than your son – and the binman comes only once a week. When Frankie does arrive he disrupts classes, he's a bad influence on the other boys, and he bullies and terrorises not just his classmates but some of the teachers also. It just can't go on. It simply can't go on.'

He looked over his glasses at this relatively young woman. She seemed a decent sort.

Agnes felt that she should say something, and her bottom lip quivered as she tried to speak. 'It's ... it's my fault ... I don't spend enough time with him at home ... he's, he's just a ... a boy.'

The principal looked over the rim of his glasses again, and he felt sad for the woman.

'I have no wish to correct you, Mrs Browne. But don't forget I also have young Dermot as a pupil here and although, yes, he is a bit of a livewire, he's a good student and a hard-working lad. I feel that he would be a better reflection of the love and care your children get at home. And, indeed, young Simon too – not the brightest, but a good solid lad.'

Agnes dropped her eyes. She didn't take compliments too well. She looked down at her hands, twisting around the strap of her handbag, then looked up at the principal again. 'So what now? What do we do now?'

'Well, Mrs Browne, I have no idea what you're going to do, but from today I am expelling your son from this school for non-attendance.'

Agnes had expected it. She didn't argue, she didn't try to appeal to the man's better nature, she simply stood and hooked her handbag over her left arm and, brushing down her coat, quietly said, 'Okay. Thank you very much,' and left.

It was a two-mile walk back to James Larkin Court for Agnes, and she cried every step of the way.

* * *

Teatime in the Browne house was storytime in many ways as each of the children fought for time to tell the highlight of their day. Cathy was all hyped up because there was to be a go-cart race down Summerhill in a week's time and she and Cathy Dowdall were going to be in it.

'They won't let youse in, youse are girls,' Dermot stated.

'So?' Cathy asked.

'Well, that's it. Youse are girls. Girls don't go into go-cart races.' Dermot knew about these things.

Cathy folded her arms in front of her and sat back in the chair, staring at Dermot. 'Says who?' she demanded.

Dermot thought for a moment. 'There's a rule somewhere. There has to be!'

'Well, there's not. And me and Cathy Dowdall are goin' into the race and what's more we're goin' to win it.'

Agnes placed a full teapot or the table and said, 'Good girl, Cathy. Who's pushin'?'

'I am,' Cathy said proudly.

'I was thinkin' so. That Cathy Dowdall wan would be too cute to have you sittin' in the go-cart and her pushin' – the lazy bitch!'

'But I *love* pushin', Ma! And I'm the fastest pusher in The Jarro.'

'Good girl, Cathy,' Mark joined in, and winked at her.

As she poured out more tea for the boys Agnes asked as offhand as she could, 'Was Frankie home this afternoon?'

Dermot was the one that answered. Very quietly, he simply said, 'No.'

Cathy piped up, 'I seen him today round the back of the shops, him and five other skinheads smokin' and drinkin' cider, Ma!'

Mark leaned across and placed his hand on Cathy's arm. 'Shush,' he said. 'Nobody likes a snitch, Cathy.'

Back at the cooker Agnes pretended she hadn't heard Cathy's remark. Before anyone had time to react to what Cathy had said Trevor strolled into the kitchen. 'Look, Ma!' he called out. He was holding ten new paintings he had done that day. He trotted over to the table and placed them on Mark's lap saying, 'Here, Marko.'

Mark feigned surprise. 'Are these for me? Wow! Thanks very much, Trevor, you're a great boy!' And he bent over and kissed the boy on the forehead. He began to flick through the pictures. 'They're very good, Trevor.'

Agnes decided to add more accolades. 'Well done, Trev. Sure, you're a great boy!'

'But they really are very good, Ma, look!' said Mark, holding up two of the pictures.

Agnes looked at the pictures and smiled. 'Yeh, they are very good. But, Jesus, I hope the teacher is not goin' to spend all her time teachin' him paintin'. That'll be no good to him – unless she teaches him a bit of wallpaper-hangin' as well.'

The children all laughed – it was a welcome reprieve from the 'Frankie' subject. When tea was over the family began to disperse, Simon and Dermot to the boys' bedroom to do their homework, Cathy to the room she shared with her mother to do press-ups. Trevor lay on the floor in the sitting-room watching TV. No homework for him! Ten paintings a day was his limit. There was just Agnes and Mark left at the tea table.

'I'm headin' out to the bingo, Mark. Listen, Rory's dinner is on the pot with a lid over it – if he's not in by quarter to eight turn the heat off underneath the pot.'

'Sure, Ma. I need a shirt and tie.'

'Ah Jaysus, Mark, you're not in court, are yeh?'

'No, I'm not,' Mark answered emphatically. 'Mr McHugh wants me to go to a meetin' with him on Monday.'

'A meetin'? For what? What kind of meetin'?'

While Agnes sipped her tea and lit yet another cigarette Mark told the story of his encounter that day with Sean McHugh. 'So now I need a bleedin' shirt and tie,' he ended.

'I'll go down to Clery's with yeh tomorrow! D'yeh know, Mark, it's no harm. You could do with a bit of decent gear. We'll get yeh the whole works. Shoes, shirt, tie, jacket, pants, the lot!'

'Steady, Ma! I'm only goin' to wear them for a day.'

'They won't go to waste, luv. Every man should have some good gear to wear.' The word 'man' had just slipped out but Mark noticed it and was very proud. Agnes stood up and began to clear off the table.

'Leave those, Ma,' Mark said. 'I'll do them. You go on to the bingo.'

'Ah, you're a sweetheart, luv.'

Agnes gathered her cigarettes and dropped them into her bingo bag, put on her coat, kissed all the children goodbye and left for the bingo.

When Rory arrived home at eight forty-five the heat under his dinner had been turned off for an hour. He had a hard job taking the lid off as it was stuck to the plate, the mashed potatoes had gone crispy and with the grease dry, the rashers now looked white.

'Ah, Jaysus, me dinner's in shite!' he exclaimed.

Mark got up from the kitchen table where he was

studying for his test and snapped the plate out of Rory's hand. 'It just needs to be heated. Here, give it to me.'

He opened the oven door, placed the plate in the rack, and using the flint spark-maker clicked the oven into life. He closed the door and stood up. 'Now! Just give it a couple of minutes in there and it'll be grand.' He went back to his books.

Rory sat down on a chair beside him. 'Oh Mark, me nerves!' Rory said, but in such a way that meant he wanted to tell a story.

Mark closed his book and placed his pencil on the table. 'Why, what's wrong with yeh?'

'I got ... I got chased home from work. I'm sweatin', and me legs are weak.'

'What? Chased? By who?'

'Skinheads. There was about ten of them. I was rattlin', Mark, yeh should have seen me. I was like Ronnie Delaney comin' up St Jarlath's Street.'

Mark was now paying great attention. Brownes don't get chased. 'Were they from here? From The Jarro?'

'I don't know – what d'yeh think I did, stopped and said can I have all your names please before I fuckin' run?'

'Take it easy. I mean, did you recognise any of them?'

'Mark, wait till I tell yeh – *they* were chasin' *me*, I wasn't chasin' them. D'yeh think I have eyes in the back of me head?'

'Okay! Just tell me where did they start chasin' yeh from?'

'Right outside Wash & Blow. I think they were waitin' for me.'

Rory got up and took a tea-towel and opened the door of the oven. Gingerly he took out the plate. 'Jesus, it's roastin'!' he yelped.

'Switch off that oven and close the door,' Mark ordered. But he wasn't thinking about the oven; he was thinking about a gang of skinheads chasing his younger brother. This wasn't on, not on at all.

Rory cut up the first of his rashers and held his hand in mid-air for Mark to see. 'Look, Mark, I'm shakin'.'

* * *

If Rory was shaking, not far away in St Francis Xavier Hall at that very moment his mother Agnes was positively vibrating.

'Top of the house – ninety.'

There was a tremor in Agnes's voice as she made the announcement to the group. 'That's it! I have a wait!'

'I don't believe yeh! What is it?' asked Carmel.

'Believe it or not, it's number seven.' Agnes sounded exasperated.

'Again? Jaysus!' groaned Nelly.

'I must be goin' to win again so,' Bunnie said rather chirpily.

'One and four – fourteen.'

'There's still a good six or seven calls to go yet, Agnes.' Carmel nudged her in the ribs.

'On its own – number seven!'

It was hard to tell at first who had actually won. Nelly, Carmel, Splish, Splash, Agnes and even Bunnie simultaneously rose to their feet and screamed 'Check!' Slightly behind Agnes and over to the left-hand side of the hall, a similar thing was taking place as another group of four or five also screamed 'Check!'

Pat Muldoon switched off his ball machine and announced, 'We seem to have a number of checks in the hall. Would everybody except the checkers please sit down and would the checkers please hold their card in the air.'

When the room had settled, there were two people left standing in the hall. Agnes looked across the room at the other checker. She knew her. It was was Pauline Dunne and she too was from The Jarro. She had five children, two of them grown up and three youngsters, and her husband had fecked off five or six years previously with the cleaner from Foley's pub. They'd gone to England. It was the talk of the area at the time. Pauline had just carried on and made a few bob for herself by filling the gap the young girl had left in Foley's, where Pauline was now a valued member of staff.

Both women were shaking. Agnes smiled nervously at Pauline and Pauline returned the smile along with a little wave.

Both checks were adjudged to be correct and the record Snowball of £620 was divided equally between the two women. To the delight of Agnes's group, the bingo organisers also gave a five-pound note to each of the five in Agnes's group and to the five people sitting around Pauline Dunne as a winning bonus. The smoked cod and chips never tasted as good as they did that night on the walk back to 92 James Larkin Court, and as if in repayment for the five-pound notes the entire group left Agnes to her front door to ensure that she got home safely. She invited them in for a cup of tea, but they all declined. As soon as she entered the flat she put the kettle on and sneaked into the boys' bedroom. She noticed Frankie's bunk was empty, then she leaned into the middle bunk and shook Mark.

'Mark, Mark, love – wake up.'

Mark woke gently. He had his back to her so he had to look over his shoulder to see who was shaking him. Once he recognised his mother he turned slowly. 'Mammy, are yeh all right?'

'I'm grand, love! Come out to the kitchen, I want to show you something.'

'Is Frankie in trouble?'

Agnes shook her head vigorously. 'No, no it's nothin' like that. I want to show you somethin' good!'

'Okay.'

'Well, come on, then.' She waited for him.

There was a moment's silence before Mark said, 'Ma, I have nothin' on me.'

Agnes jumped. 'Oh sorry, love. I'll be in the kitchen. I'll make a cup of tea. Follow me out.'

Agnes made a swift exit, reflecting on her way how short the time was between a younger Mark saying, 'Mammy, why have I got hair on me willie?' and now, 'Mammy, wait outside, I've nothing on.' It seemed to have been particularly short for Mark.

Mark was still a bit groggy when he came into the kitchen, though his eyes opened wide when he saw the six huge fifty-pound notes and the tenner spread across the table. He froze and stared at them. Then it dawned on him. 'You won the fuckin' Snowball!'

'Mind your language, son!'

'Sorry, Ma. Congratulations!'

He took her in his arms and snuggling his nose between her earlobe and her neck squeezed her tightly. Agnes closed her eyes and thought he might look like a man, he might talk like a man, but he still hugged her like a child.

Mark sat down and began to drink the tea his mother had made. For a while the two of them just sat in silence staring at the money.

'Three hundred and ten pounds!' Mark said, and he giggled.

'Yeh!' Agnes giggled too.

'What are yeh goin' to do with it, Ma?'

'I don't know. Yeh don't think I've just been sittin' around plannin' how to spend the Snowball, do yeh?'

They heard the letterbox open and both of them looked at the door. Frankie's nicotine-stained fingers poked in and wrapped around the piece of wool that held the door key. Slowly the key began to rise until it disappeared out the letterbox. Quickly Agnes gathered up the money and moved to the sink where her handbag was. She had the money put away and the handbag snapped shut before the front door opened. Frankie closed the door and pulled the key back in the letterbox. As he entered the kitchen he was a bit startled to find Agnes and Mark sitting drinking tea. Agnes looked him straight in the face. Mark turned his head away and looked at his mug of tea.

'What's up?' Frankie asked. There was a touch of a slur in his words.

Agnes seized the opportunity. 'I'll tell you what's up, son! The game is up – for you!'

'What d'yeh mean?'

'You've been expelled from school.'

'Big deal – so what?'

Mark's head snapped up from his tea. 'Don't speak to Mammy like that!' His voice was even but firm.

Frankie held his gaze for a few moments, then backed down. Skinhead or not, Frankie had no intention of mixing it with the biggest seventeen-year-old in The Jarro. He began to shift from leg to leg uneasily.

'I hated that school anyway. The teachers picked on me every chance they got.'

'Well, from the amount of times you've been in school they've had precious little chance,' said Agnes.

Mark went back to staring at his tea. He had often seen Agnes give Frankie a dressing-down before. Sometimes he felt they were just for his benefit, a kind of mock telling-off. Frankie would apologise and tomorrow it would all be forgotten. Frankie would then return to doing his own thing in his own way until the next dressing-down.

Agnes lit a cigarette. As she blew out the match and placed it in the ashtray, Frankie went to walk past the kitchen table to the bedroom.

'Where are yeh goin'?' Agnes asked him.

He stopped and half-turned. 'To bed,' he replied in a tone that suggested she shouldn't be asking him such stupid questions.

'I'm not finished yet.' She took a sip of tea.

Frankie turned back to face his mother. 'Go on, then,' he said, ready now to endure the rest of the routine.

'Here's the deal, Francis.' Now she looked him straight in the eye. 'Now that you're outa school you have two weeks to get yourself a job and start bringin' in some money to this house.'

'Or else?' Frankie asked, tryin' to hurry things up.

'I'll tell yeh or else, Mister! Or else yeh find yourself somewhere else to live!'

Slowly Mark raised his head from his mug of tea to look at his mother. He couldn't believe his ears, but he knew from the look on her face that she was deadly serious.

Agnes went on. 'The only people in this house who don't pay their way are those who are bein' educated. Now, if you don't want to be educated that's fine, get a job and pay your way, or else – out.' She jerked her thumb in the direction of the door.

Frankie stared at her speechless, then made to reply, but before he could Agnes simply said, 'Good night, Francis,' and took another drag of her cigarette.

Frankie stumbled into the bedroom, reeling from the shock of Agnes's pronouncement.

Mark stared at his mother. She was shaking and her eyes were filling up. She caught Mark's look and as if by way of explanation she said, 'If it was just me I wouldn't mind, Mark. But I'm not havin' the entire household upset by one bastard. It took me fourteen years to get rid of the last one!' She stubbed out her cigarette.

Mark still stared at her. 'You wouldn't,' he simply said.

Agnes stood up and said very firmly, 'You bloody watch me!'

Chapter 4

THE NEXT DAY, SATURDAY, AS PROMISED, Agnes took Mark down to Clery's. Having never bought a suit for himself before, Mark of course didn't know which way to look or what to try. Agnes herself couldn't be described as a slave to fashion, but from her dates with Pierre she had picked up enough from looking at how he dressed to know what looks good on a man. She chose a white cotton tailor-fit shirt, a pair of beige cavalry twill trousers, a grey and wine striped tie and what can only be described as a double-breasted blazer, in the style of the Beatles, with its high, up-turned wing-style collar. It was wine with gold buttons. Agnes insisted on paying for the ensemble, and the lot cost her just over £35. Mark argued with her, insisting that he pay the bill as he had over £60 saved, but Agnes stuck to her guns, delighted to treat Mark to his first business-meeting outfit. However, she did let him pay for the shoes himself. He chose a pair of all-leather Blackthorn brogues, which alone cost £11.

Meanwhile up in Henry Street, young Dermot was doing a little bit of shopping of his own. Just a bit of gear he needed to keep his wardrobe up-to-date. Unlike Mark with his savings, or Agnes with her bingo win, Dermot hadn't a penny to his name. He was out for an afternoon's shoplifting.

He decided on a pair of navy-blue corduroy trousers in Arnott's. His plan was simple. He wandered through the store for about thirty minutes before stealing his first item. This was an empty brown-paper bag with the words 'Arnott's Store Dublin' written across it. Armed with this, he went to the boys' section where he picked out a pair of brown corduroy trousers in his own size, 26inch waist. Dermot was an independent shopper, he had his own methods. He folded the trousers carefully and slipped them into the Arnott's bag, and then made his way straight to the Security Man at the main door. Dermot tipped the man on the arm and the Security Man turned around and looked down at the blond-haired, blue-eyed boy with the babyish smile, who looked like an innocent twelve-year-old.

'Excuse me, Mister, are you the manager?' Dermot asked, full of innocence.

'No, I'm the store security, son. What do you want the manager for?' the man asked, still trying to keep an eye on the store.

Dermot opened the bag to reveal the folded pair of brown corduroy trousers. He looked into the bag himself and held it open for the Security Man to peep in also.

'It's these, Mister,' he said.

The man looked into the bag and was a little confused. 'What about them?'

'Me Mammy got them this mornin''. They should be blue not brown. And she sent me up to change them.'

'Come with me, son.' The Security Man spoke as if he were the manager. He walked Dermot up to one of the cash points at the men's and boys' section and drew one of the young ladies aside.

'Excuse me, love. If you've got time would you look after him for me. I've got to get back to the door.'

'Sure, Tom. What is it, dear?'

Dermot proffered the bag. 'I need to change these to navy.'

'Certainly, dear. Do you have a receipt?'

'Daddy said I didn't need a receipt.'

'Daddy?'

'Yeh, Daddy.' Dermot pointed at the retreating Security Man.

'Oh, you're Tom's little boy!'

Dermot opened his blue eyes as wide as he could, smiled and nodded his head.

'Of course, dear, come along with me. So tell me, which one are you, Barry or John?'

'Barry,' Dermot lied, and very convincingly.

* * *

After leaving Clery's, both pretty pleased with themselves, Agnes and Mark crossed the street to the GPO and began to stroll up Henry Street to do some window-shopping. They talked about Rory, and how well he was doing at Wash & Blow. Mark told Agnes how excited he was about attending the meeting this coming Monday with Mr McHugh and yet how frightened he was at the same time. They discussed the move to Finglas and what it would mean to the family. They even talked about the two Cathys' chances of winning the go-cart race the following Saturday. They talked about everything and anything – except Frankie. As they passed the entrance to Arnott's upstairs café the aroma of freshly brewed coffee and freshly cooked pastries wafted out the door.

'Mmm,' said Agnes, 'd'yeh fancy a coffee, Mark?'

'Yeh, yeh sure, Ma. Well, tea, actually.'

And up the stairs they went. Agnes took the shopping bags from Mark as he went to the self-service counter to get the drinks and cakes. She wandered around the seating area looking for a table where they could have a little bit of privacy, not easy to find on a Saturday afternoon. She eventually settled on a side-booth. She placed the bags on the bench seat on the right-hand side and slid herself into the bench seat on the left-hand side.

From where Agnes sat she had a fine view of the store. Boy, is it busy, she thought. There were people milling in every direction. It was the little blond head bobbing along the racks that caught her eye – that tends to happen when you have seven children and five of them are blond. She followed the head with her eyes as it bobbed along a rail of Holy Communion jackets, then as the figure emerged she could clearly see that it was indeed her own little Dermot. He was chatting away to one of the sales assistants and they seemed to be getting on great.

Just then Mark arrived with the tray. 'Here we go, Ma. I got you a chocolate éclair and I got a cream slice for meself,' he announced.

'Mark, isn't that our Dermot down there in the boys' section?'

Mark placed one knee on the bench seat and stretched over to the balcony to look down. 'Where, Ma? I don't see anythin'.'

Agnes now stood and pointed over to the boys' section. 'There. Look, talkin' to the young one.'

'Oh jayney yeh, that's Dermo all right,' Mark confirmed.

'What's he doin' in here? And what's in that bag he's carryin'?'

Mark had a sinking feeling and his stomach tightened. He tried to think as quickly as he could. 'I don't know ... eh ... Oh yeh, he said somethin' earlier on about goin' down to Henry Street for a message for Mrs Egan, maybe that's it?'

Agnes was still looking down at Dermot. 'Must be. Ah, fair play to him, he's a good lad! He'd do a run for anyone.'

* * *

The girl was most helpful. She obviously liked Tom and his 'son' got the red-carpet treatment. Dermot thanked the lady and again made his way back to Tom, the Security Man. He tugged his jacket. Tom turned around.

'Well, son, did you get fixed up?' Tom asked.

'Yes, Mister, thanks very much.'

As he said this, Dermot glanced back at the sales lady. As he suspected, she was staring directly at the pair of them. Dermot looked up at the Security Man and said, 'Mister, can I tell yeh a secret?'

The Security Man smiled. ''Course yeh can, son,' and he stooped over.

Dermot placed his arms around the man's neck and whispered in his ear. 'I still wet the bed.'

The man looked straight into the boy's face, puzzled, and then replied, 'Ah, that's no harm, son, you'll grow out of that,' and he patted Dermot on the head.

From where the sales assistant was standing, it looked like Tom had just received a hug from his son. She was touched. Dermot once again looked in her direction and still she stood, looking at the pair. Dermot said to Tom, pointing at the girl, 'That girl was really nice.'

Tom looked in the direction of Dermot's pointed finger and then Dermot waved at the girl. The girl waved back and for some reason, unknown to himself, even Tom waved. Tom then got back to business. 'Okay, son, you're fixed up now. Off you go.'

Dermot started to move away, then turned and said, 'Thanks a lot,' and then just to himself he added 'Daddy,' and laughed as he left the store richer by one pair of corduroy trousers.

* * *

Agnes gave Mark a running commentary on the whole scene. Mark didn't look – he couldn't bear to look.

'He's leavin' yer woman now. Jaysus, yeh'd think they were best friends.' She took a quick sup of coffee and a bite of chocolate éclair. 'Now he's talkin' to the bloody Security Man.'

Mark paled. 'Did the Security Man call him over?' Mark asked nervously.

Without turning around to Mark, Agnes answered. 'No, Dermot just walked straight over to him.' Another sup of coffee. 'Jaysus!' Agnes exclaimed.

'What?'

'He's huggin' the Security Man!'

'Maybe – maybe he knows him, Ma,' Mark offered.

'Ah Jaysus, Mark. I know the girl at the checkout in Power's Supermarket but yeh don't see me huggin' her.' She tugged Mark's sleeve.

'Ah, yeh have to see this, Mark! Yer woman is wavin' down the shop and Dermot and the Security Man are wavin' back – it's like somethin' out of *The Sound of* bleedin' *Music.*'

Mark couldn't take any more of this. He knelt up on the seat. 'Where are they, Ma?'

Agnes turned back to her coffee. 'Too late, luv, he's gone. I wonder what that was all about?'

'I wonder?' Mark said, and went back to his cream bun and tea, relieved in the knowledge that Dermot hadn't been caught – yet!

* * *

Saturday evening after tea the Browne household was very busy as everybody rushed to prepare for their night's entertainment. Since he had begun working and got his very first wage packet, Rory had taken Dermot and Simon to the pictures every Saturday evening. Every second Saturday night Cathy would go down to Cathy Dowdall's flat and stay overnight with her, and on alternate nights the two would stay in the Brownes'. Tonight it was Cathy Browne's turn to travel the couple of blocks down the road, so she was packing her toothbrush and nightie.

Agnes had her bath and got herself ready for her weekly date with Pierre. What had got off to a rocky start three years ago had now become a firm friendship of sorts. They held hands and often kissed fondly, but it always ended there. There was absolutely no sex. In fairness to Pierre, it wasn't for the want of trying, and Agnes came close a couple of times – but something always went wrong at the last minute and Agnes would chicken out. It was also a question of facilities. Pierre still shared the living accommodation above his uncle's Pizza Parlour with his uncle and two cousins, so they couldn't go there, and needless to say a few quiet moments in the Browne home was absolutely out of the question. This reduced the possibilities to Pierre's car, a Fiat 127 – no chance! Or to booking a hotel room. This they had tried once.

It was a newly opened hotel in Drumcondra, The Skylon. Pierre suggested that he and Agnes have a drink there to see what it was like, and he also told her that when they got there he would have a surprise for her. For the life of her, Agnes couldn't think what the surprise would be, so she arrived at the hotel with Pierre, full of anticipation and not a little excited. When Pierre revealed what the surprise was – that he had booked a room in the hotel for the night – Agnes was shocked, at first! But after three bottles of cider she thought the idea hilarious and began to rib Pierre for even thinking of it! Three more bottles of cider and Agnes, now becoming a little amorous, wasn't so sure that this might not be a good idea. It took just one more bottle to convince her. Pierre was thrilled.

'When you finish that bottle, we will go upstairs, yes?'

'Don't be ridiculous, Pierre,' Agnes snapped at him as she glanced around the room to see if there was anybody she knew there.

'But, my darling, I thought you said yes?'

'I did say yes, but we can't make it so obvious.'

'Well, then, what shall we do, my darling?'

Agnes thought for a moment and came up with a plan. 'I'll go into the ladies' toilet. When I'm gone in you go on up to the room on your own, like you were a businessman goin' to bed. Then when I come out of the ladies' I'll finish me glass of cider and I'll go into the lift on me own and go up to the room.'

Pierre thought about this for a moment and, although he thought it was silly – and were they in France and Agnes a French woman it would have been – he was prepared to go along with any plan as long as it meant getting Agnes up to that room. So he agreed.

'Okay, my darling. The room is 213, on floor two.'

'Gotcha – 213 on floor two.'

Pierre stood and stretched his arms, and looking around gave an exaggerated yawn, then quite loudly announced, 'Oh dear! I am such a tired businessman. I think I shall go to bed.'

Agnes looked at him aghast. 'What are yeh doin', yeh gobshite? You're not in a play! Just fuck off to bed, will yeh?' she whispered hoarsely.

Quickly and without reply, Pierre scurried out of the lounge and into the lift. Agnes, in the meantime, headed for the ladies' toilet. She felt a little woozy, so she went to the sink and splashed cold water on her face. This freshened her up a bit, but it also removed some of her make-up, so she re-applied the 'war paint', then, satisfied with her reflection, she left the ladies' and went back to her drink. As she was drinking, her eyes moved from right to left around the room and when the glass was empty she very casually rose and, steadily and very nonchalantly, walked to the lift, pressed the button and entered. The doors closed, and Agnes looked at the numbered floor buttons. Aloud she said, 'Now 213 on the first floor – no on the second floor – or was it 321? Oh Jesus, what's the number?'

Suddenly the lift doors slid open and Agnes jumped with fright. An American gentleman stepped in and asked, 'Going up?'

'Gettin' out,' replied Agnes, and left in a hurry.

She returned to her seat and tried to think what to do next. The waitress came over and Agnes ordered another bottle of cider.

Fifteen minutes later, while Agnes was still sitting in the lounge sipping her glass of cider, the 'phone behind the bar rang. The barman picked it up.

'Hello. Bar.'

'Hello. I wonder could you do me a favour?'

'Certainly, sir. If I can.'

'Sitting in the lounge is a very beautiful dark-haired lady.'

The barman looked around. 'Eh yes, sir, I can see her from here.'

'Would you ask her to join Pierre in his room – that's room 213 as soon as she is ready?'

'Well, sir, I'm not sure if I'm allowed – '

But Pierre interrupted him. 'No, of course I understand, but this is okay. The lady is expecting this call.'

The barman thought about it for a moment and then said, 'Oh well, in that case, sir, I'll tell the lady.'

Agnes watched the barman as he spoke on the 'phone. Suddenly he was looking around the lounge. He then stooped down to go out of a hatch beneath the bar into the lounge proper. He walked straight over towards Agnes. When he got about five feet from her, he nodded and smiled, she nodded and smiled back – and he walked straight past her. The barman carried on to another table just a little bit away from where Agnes was sitting. He sat down and spoke to a dark-haired woman. Whatever he was saying made the lady look very serious, then she smiled, thanked him, put her cigarettes and lighter into her handbag and left the lounge. Agnes then lost interest. She had finally figured out what to do. She would go out to the reception desk and simply ask what room Mr Pierre du Gloss was residing in.

She finished the last of her cider and made her way out. The receptionist, although very friendly, explained that it was not hotel policy to give out room numbers on request. But she said she could put Agnes through on the phone to Mr du Gloss's room. Agnes was happy with this, and the lady pointed to a phone booth across the lobby in which Agnes could take the call. Agnes entered the booth and closed the door. She sat on the small stool and suddenly the white 'phone in front of her burst into life. She picked up the 'phone. The receptionist said, 'You're through to that room now.'

Agnes thanked her. There was a slight click and she heard the phone ringing. It rang and rang and rang. There was no reply. Agnes let it ring until the receptionist eventually cut in and announced, 'I'm sorry, there's no reply from that room.'

Again Agnes thanked her and replaced the receiver. She sat for a moment, wondering what to do, then through the glass door of the booth she saw Pierre being led through the lobby in handcuffs by female detective Jacintha Doody of the Dublin Metropolitan Vice Squad. The case never came to court and Pierre was let off with a very stiff warning.

* * *

As she checked herself over in the mirror for this Saturday night's date Agnes giggled to herself at the memory of that most eventful night.

Apart from Trevor, the only member of the Browne household who wasn't going out that night was Mark. Mark would stay in and baby-sit Trevor, as he did every Saturday night. Agnes often worried about Mark's lack of social life, but figured that Mark would do his own thing when he was ready.

As it turned out, her date that night would be a short one, as Pierre had to get back to the Pizza Parlour early to help with the after-pub rush. Agnes wasn't too disappointed because she would be home in time to see the last half, and usually the best part, of *The Late Late Show* with Gay Byrne.

When everyone had gone out and Trevor had finally gone off to sleep, Mark opened up his text books and began to study for his upcoming test. Tonight he was reading about the use of pulpwoods in the manufacture of furniture. Plywoods, blockboard and chipboard were becoming the base materials in the upholstered furniture manufacturing business. This is of no use to me, thought Mark. He likened it to learning Irish in school – so much effort went into learning something he would not be using once school was over. Wise & Company specialised in hardwood and leather furniture. This was Mark's forte. Still, he had to study this area because there would be questions on it in the test. 'No knowledge ever goes to waste,' Mr Wise had said to him, even though Mr Wise was the one who scoffed at the idea of pulpwood frames for furniture.

But Mark's thoughts were not totally on plywoods. He could not get Betty Collins off his mind. On the way back from their shopping trip that day, Agnes had suggested that Mark take the new pants up to Maggie Collins in

Gardiner Row. Maggie had been a seamstress in her younger years and now made a steady few bob by doing alterations from her home. Mark's pants were about an inch too long, and Maggie, Agnes told him, would take them up in a jiffy.

He found the building, Number 32, easily. Maggie had the ground-floor flat and as he knocked on the door Mark could hear the mechanical 'rat, tat, tat,' of the Singer sewing machine from behind the door. The door was opened by a woman of about forty, with hair dyed platinum blond.

'I need a pair of trousers taken up,' Mark said, without introducing himself.

'Come in, son,' Maggie invited, and stood back to allow Mark to enter. He stepped into the flat. Despite the fact that Maggie herself had opened the door and was now standing before him, Mark could still hear the sewing machine busily working away in an adjoining room. There was a beautiful aroma in the flat that could only come from sausages frying.

'Show me the pants, love.' Maggie took the bag. She unfolded the pants and looked at the bottom of the legs. 'Turn-ups,' she mused and then cried, 'Betty!'

Mark jumped.

Suddenly the machine in the other room stopped, the door opened and out walked Maggie's daughter, Betty.

'Yeh?' Betty asked, not looking at Mark.

'Pair of pants with turn-ups. Run them up, love, will yeh? I'm in the middle of the dinner.'

She threw the pants to the young girl. Betty still had not looked at Mark. But Mark had not taken his eyes off her. She was tall, for a girl, only just shorter than Mark, though she was two years older at nineteen. She had dark skin, brown eyes and the most beautiful white teeth Mark had ever seen. This was not the first time Mark had laid eyes on Betty Collins. Up to three years ago Mark would often see her at the parish hall. He would be doing his football training in the waste ground beside the hall and she would arrive dressed in the black beret and suit of the Irish Red Cross. What stunned him at this moment was that at that time Betty Collins seemed to be one of the least attractive girls he had ever seen. Now she stood there, a vision of beauty!

She looked at him. 'Oh! It's you. Hi, Mark!' She smiled.

'Eh, yeh. How' yeh?' Mark reddened.

'What's your leg measurement?' she asked.

'Me leg? Why?' Mark was flustered.

The girl laughed. 'I have to know how much to take up.'

'I don't know – they just need about that much.' Mark held up his hand with the finger and thumb about an inch apart.

She shrieked with laughter and from her back pocket took a rolled-up measuring tape. Now *she* blushed. She unrolled the tape and fingered it. Then she quickly vanished into the kitchen. Mark shoved his hands into his pockets and shuffled his feet. The sound of the two women mumbling was followed by a loud laugh from Maggie. Seconds later, Maggie came from the kitchen with a cigarette butt in her mouth, holding the measuring tape.

'Right, son, open your legs!' Mark did. Coughing and laughing simultaneously, Maggie measured his inside leg at thirty-four inches.

From where he stood waiting, Mark could see in

through the half-open door. Betty rocked forward each time she ran the material through the machine. She was wearing a tartan man's shirt with the sleeves rolled up, the front and tail hanging over her jeans. The top three buttons of the shirt were open and each time she bent forward, Mark caught sight of the top of her breast and the lacy rim of a snow-white bra. He felt warm and clammy. His heart thumped and his stomach heaved. Yet he didn't want to be anywhere else in the world.

* * *

By the time Agnes arrived home that night from her date the boys had returned from the pictures and were in bed, though not before Mark had taken Dermot to one side and warned him of the consequences of being caught shoplifting. Agnes hadn't even noticed the pair of blue corduroy slacks Dermot had on him that night. Dermot appeared to take this telling off on the chin, but secretly, like all thieves, he thought that he would never be caught.

Chapter 5

THE SHIRT COLLAR AROUND MARK'S NECK felt tight and agitated him. He had already endured the wolf whistles of the early morning 'auld wans' sweeping down the steps of their buildings as he walked through The Jarro. He had tried to hold a steady smile, but knew that his face was so red it nearly matched the wine-coloured jacket.

It was Mary Cullen who spotted him first and she attracted the attention of two other neighbours, Mrs Williams and Mrs Troy. 'Hey, girls!' she cried. 'Would you look who it is, Michael fuckin' Caine! "What's It All About, Alfie",' she began to sing.

The other two women screamed with laughter and joined in the jeers.

'Hey, Mark!' Mrs Williams called. 'Would you risk it for a biscuit?'

'Go on outa that, Mark Browne,' Mrs Troy called, 'wiggle your arse when you go by us, yeh fine thing!'

It wasn't until he rounded the corner into Cathal Brugha Street and saw his reflection in a shop window that he realised how well he actually looked. He even caught one or two girls, standing at bus stops, giving him that longer-than-usual look, and began to enjoy it! Finally he was outside the Gresham hotel, his stomach churning with a mixture of nerves and excitement. At last he caught sight of Sean McHugh as he waddled his way up O'Connell Street. The bald, short man with stumpy legs and an arse as big as a doormat met Mark with a beaming smile.

'Well, if it isn't Paul Newman,' Sean chuckled.

'Ah stop, Mr McHugh. I feel ridiculous,' Mark answered shyly.

'Well, you look great! Just like a proper executive, young Mr Browne,'

Sean put his arm around Mark's waist as he guided him up the steps of the Gresham hotel. This made Mark feel good, a little more secure.

'Did you call into Mr Wise this morning?' Mark enquired.

'I did, yeh, I did. I've only just left him. I told him you were coming with me and he was delighted,' enthused Sean.

'How is he, Mr McHugh?'

'Not great, Mark, not great at all.'

They crossed the lobby of the hotel, Sean McHugh glancing from table to table. Two gentlemen in suits sitting at a table just outside the restaurant door stood up and the older of the two waved in their direction. Mark poked Sean.

'Over there, Mr McHugh. Is that them?'

Sean returned the wave enthusiastically and advanced towards the two men. He took the older man's hand firmly and with genuine warmth in his voice said, 'Ah, Greg, good to see you. Welcome to Dublin!' He turned to Mark. 'Greg, I'd like you to meet Mark Browne, one of the new young bloods in Wise & Company. Mark, this is Greg

Smyth, Managing Director of our longest-standing customer, Smyth & Blythe.'

As he said this he looked straight into the eyes of Greg Smyth. Greg was uncomfortable. The younger man with him was introduced as Frank Reel, accountant for Smyth & Blythe. The four sat down and while Greg and Sean exchanged a little banter, mostly concerning Mr Wise's health, the accountant waved to a waitress to order some refreshments.

Frank Reel had without consultation with the rest of the company ordered coffee for four. Mark had never drunk coffee before. He took the odd cup of tea, maybe one or two cups a day, but wasn't overly fond of the stuff. The coffee arrived on a silver tray and after signing the bill Frank poured out four cups. Mark had no idea what way coffee should be taken, so he watched Frank and repeated Frank's every move. Frank dropped two lumps of sugar into his coffee, Mark dropped two lumps of sugar into his. Frank poured cream into his coffee, Mark poured cream into his. He even stirred his coffee as long as Frank had stirred his. Then Mark took his first mouthful. To his great surprise he loved it! As soon as everybody had taken a mouthful of coffee and Greg and Sean had lit cigarettes, the pleasantries were over and they got down to business.

Mark listened intently. Greg Smyth and his accountant were like a double act – they spoke uninterrupted for twenty minutes solid. Mark heard phrases like 'market forces', 'purchasing fluctuations', 'expendability', 'volume selling', none of which he understood. He did understand the thrust of where these two men were leading. Wise & Co. were about to lose a customer. Not once, Mark noted, did he hear the words 'quality', 'class' or 'reliability'. These were three words Mr Wise had taught Mark in his very first week that were the essence of good furniture. At the end of the speech there was a short – a very short – pause when the two men looked at each other. Then Greg eventually said, 'So you can see, Sean, that we can no longer carry on the way we are. I deeply regret having to do this, but we will not be placing any more orders with Wise & Co.' He opened a folder and took out a white envelope which he handed to Sean. 'This, I believe, will bring our account up to date. I'm sorry, Sean.' And he sounded genuinely sorry.

Sean just nodded and placed the envelope in his inside pocket. He exhaled a deep sigh and was obviously about to speak, but before he could, Mark interjected with, 'Why not?'

Greg Smyth looked at Mark as if he had seen him for the very first time. 'I beg your pardon?'

Mark looked to Sean to see if he was upsetting him in any way by taking part in the conversation. Sean's face was expressionless, so Mark returned his gaze to Greg Smyth. 'Why will yeh not be placing any more orders with us?'

It was the accountant who answered. 'Mark, nobody wants expensive furniture anymore. Today's furniture has nearly become disposable. People nowadays want to be able to change their furniture as often as they change their wallpaper. So the new trend is not quality hand-carved leather chairs that are expensive, it's colourful, modern three-piece suites that are cheap. That's the way the market is going; that's the way we have to go.'

Mark did not answer but nodded in understanding. The two older men stood up, indicating that the meeting was now at an end. They all shook hands and Sean and Mark left the Gresham. As they walked slowly down O'Connell Street, Mark said, 'You knew that was comin', didn't yeh?'

'Aye.'

'Is losing Smyth & Blythe bad for us?'

'Really bad, Mark. It could be the final straw.'

They walked in silence for a couple of hundred yards, then Sean sighed and said, 'I'm not looking forward to telling Mr Wise.'

Mark stopped and put his arm on Sean McHugh's shoulder. 'Then don't tell him, Mr McHugh,' he exclaimed.

'What? Sure, I have to.'

'Not yet,' Mark said. 'Just give me one day before you tell him! Please, Mr McHugh, I have an idea.'

Sean looked into Mark's face and in Mark's eyes he saw something familiar. There was a fire of defiance, a refusal to believe that no matter how bad the situation was that it could not be changed. Sean McHugh had seen it before, twice. The first time was in the eyes of his hero and Commander-in-chief, Michael Collins; the second time was in 1933 in the eyes of a much younger Mr Wise. Quietly and simply, he said, 'Okay.'

Mark smiled. 'You go on back to the factory, Mr McHugh. I'll be back a bit later, I've gotta go and see me Mammy first.'

* * *

It had been a quiet morning in Moore Street market, so Agnes had used the opportunity to slip into Christy's bargain store and get herself an airmail writing pad and envelopes. It took her nearly two hours to write the letter to her sister Dolly in Canada. She'd write a couple of lines, then serve a customer, then write a couple more lines. She opened the letter with news of her great bingo Snowball win, padded it out with news of the boys and Cathy and how they were all doing. She told Dolly about the move to Finglas that now looked like it would take place within the next few weeks, and then she closed with the suggestion that now that she had a few bob to her name she might visit Dolly this summer and take young Trevor with her. She sealed and addressed the envelope, then gave Liam the Sweeper two shillings to get an airmail stamp and post the letter.

Agnes was more than surprised to see Mark suddenly standing at her stall on the other side of the rosy red apples.

'What are you doin' here?' she exclaimed.

'I need to talk to yeh, Mammy,' he said gravely.

'Is there somethin' up with one of the chisellers?' Agnes asked, worried.

'No, no, Ma, nothin' like that. Have yeh a minute?'

The other stall holders were screaming. 'Yoo hoo! Who's the fine thing down there, Agnes?'

Winnie the Mackerel yelled across, 'Hey, Mark, yeh bleedin' ride! Take me, I'm yours.' She rolled her eyes. This was greeted with a howl of laughter around the stalls. Not that anyone in their right mind would ever dream in a moment of insanity of 'taking' Winnie the Mackerel, for Winnie was only short of a white tooth for a snooker set.

Agnes let a roar at them. 'Go on outa that, ye'r embarrassin' the chap.' But really she was pleased at the reaction and proud of her son who in his new outfit could have been a film star out of Hollywood. She smiled at Mark. 'Come on around this side of the stall, love, and we'll have a chat.'

Mark made his way around to the back of stall and Agnes pulled up an empty case for him to sit on. She sat on her milk crate. 'So, what's up, love?'

'I need to borrow fifty pounds off yeh, Ma.'

'Fifty pounds? Jaysus! Am I allowed to ask what it's for?' Agnes was taken aback.

'Of course yeh are, but honestly, Ma, if I was to take the time to tell yeh the whole story the two of us would have beards.' Quickly he gave her the broad outline of the situation. 'The bottom line is I'm gonna try somethin' that I hope will help Mr Wise hang on to this valuable customer,' he finished. 'Now, I have fifty pounds meself, but I need another fifty to get what I need.' He waited expectantly.

Agnes asked no more questions. In his seventeen years Mark had never asked Agnes for one single penny. Mind you, to start with fifty pounds was a bit of a shocker, but her faith and trust in the young man was infinite. She delved into her handbag and withdrew a fifty-pound note.

Mark's eyes opened wide. 'Jesus, Ma, I didn't expect you to have it here and now. Don't tell me you're carrying that money around with yeh all the time?'

'Nah, I just put that fifty in me bag 'cause it made me feel good. Yeh know, walkin' around town with fifty quid in your bag, it's a nice feelin'. I have the rest hid at home in one of me suede boots in the wardrobe.'

'Good – and keep it hid,' Mark said emphatically.

Mark took the fifty-pound note, kissed his mother on the cheek and was off about his very important business. He went to the Browne flat in James Larkin Court where he picked up his own fifty pounds. He took out a blank work pad and pencil, and spent his morning sketching page after page. In a few hours he had finished three different designs for three suites of furniture.

* * *

'We should use a rope!' exclaimed Cathy Browne. She was sitting on the tiny wall that surrounded Mountjoy Square, using the railings as a back rest. She had her elbows on her knees and her head was cupped in her hands. She was wearing a serious look of contemplation as she stared at the go-cart. Written on the side of the cart was 'Flippin' Flyer'. Sitting beside her in an identical pose was her best friend and driver Cathy Dowdall.

'Nah! I'll use me feet. I'm better steerin' with me feet.'

'I'll tell yeh what.' Cathy Browne stood up. 'We'll try one run with the rope and then we'll try one with your feet and we'll see which is the fastest – okay?'

Cathy Dowdall was impressed with this suggestion and between them they began fixing the rope to the front axle. When it was firmly in place they pulled the cart over to the top of Fitzgibbon Street, the site of next Saturday's go-cart race. The course would run from the traffic lights to a white chalked line that would be drawn just past Fitzgibbon Street police station.

Cathy Dowdall climbed on board and gripped the rope tightly, lacing it through her fingers as if she were holding the reins of a thoroughbred stallion. Cathy Browne stood behind her, hands placed firmly on the other Cathy's shoulders and a look of fierce concentration on her face – like she was going to have a shite any minute.

'Ready – steady – go!' Cathy Dowdall screamed, and with a huge grunt Cathy Browne launched the cart.

Flippin' Flyer was living up to its name and making

great speed down Fitzgibbon Street. Cathy Dowdall had her eyes squinted up and her tongue sticking out one side of her mouth, and was crouched down in a pose of grim determination. For a brief moment she wondered what the object was as it flew past her on her right-hand side. When she heard the loud scraping sound and saw Cathy Browne tumble head-over-heels, she quickly realised it was one of her back wheels. The cart slewed sideways off the footpath, throwing Cathy Dowdall into the gutter. The cart proceeded down the hill, flipping over and over, as splinters of wood flew in all directions. It came to a sudden halt at a post which held a sign that warned of an oncoming junction. There was a loud bang and the body of the cart snapped in half.

The two girls rose slowly to their feet. They were standing thirty feet apart. Cathy Browne had blood streaming from her knee-cap, and a strip of material hung down from her torn skirt. Cathy Dowdall was in a worse state. Both her knees and both elbows were bleeding, and blood trickled from a cut just above her left eye. She stood staring at the debris that was once the Flippin' Flyer, her bottom lip quivering in her pale face. She turned to look at Cathy Browne. She too stood, hands by her sides in shock, tiny rivulets of tears running down her cheeks.

* * *

Mark arrived back at Wise & Co. at 3pm. Although he was wearing his work clothes, instead of going straight to his bench he went to Sean McHugh's office. There he outlined what he intended to do and made two requests of Sean. One was for the rest of the afternoon off, the other was for the keys of the factory, so he could return after six o'clock when everyone had gone home. As he handed over the keys, Sean McHugh shook his head, astonished at the young man's enthusiasm.

'I wish I had your energy, young Mark Browne. You'll have your own factory some day, I'm sure of it!'

Mark took the keys with a smile and replied, 'Maybe you're right, Mr McHugh. But when I do I hope I'm lucky enough to get a foreman like Mr Wise has here.' He winked at the old man, dropped the keys into his pocket and headed off for his afternoon's shopping.

His first port of call was Noyek's timber yard in Parnell Street. Here he purchased four sheets of eight-foot by four-foot half-inch marine plywood and ten ten-foot lengths of two-by-two rough deal. The lot cost him £26 and Mark wrote this amount down in his notebook. It was important for him to keep track of exactly how much this exercise was going to cost. The company agreed to deliver the timber to Wise & Co. within the hour. It was only a ten-minute walk from there to Zhivago Upholstery Supplies in Capel Street. It took some time to pick out what he needed here, mainly because of his inexperience. He looked first at the covering materials. Trying to visualise the finished product in his head, he eventually chose a light tan leatherette, and two moquettes, one mink grey and the other whiskey brown. He needed twenty yards of each and at nineteen shillings a yard this represented his biggest outlay of £57. For seat cushions Zhivago had a choice of four-inch or five-inch thickness. There was a shilling in the difference. Mark figured the extra fifteen shillings was worth it, and took fifteen of the five-inch cushions. He then chose forty yards of one-and-a-half-inch foam sheeting at three shillings a yard. This cost him

£6. Other small miscellaneous items, like wax thread, circular needles, and a hundred button shells, cost him a further £1/15/–. Again the company agreed to deliver to Wise & Co. before closing time at half-past five. Mark's total spend was £96/10/–. His shopping done, Mark arrived home for his tea with the family at quarter-past five. As soon as he had finished his tea the work would begin.

As he entered the flat, Agnes came from the kitchen to meet him in the hallway.

'Well, how did yeh do?' she asked.

'Ninety-six pounds ten shillings,' Mark said simply.

'Jaysus! Did yeh get it all?'

Mark crossed his fingers before he answered. 'I hope so.'

Just then Cathy came tearing out of the bedroom and flung her arms around Mark's waist. She was sobbing. He lifted her up. 'Hey, hey, hey! What's the matter with my princess?'

'The Flippin' Flyer,' Cathy sobbed. 'It's dead!'

'That feckin' go-cart! Look at her knees – now she'll never be a model!' Agnes said as she went back to the cooker.

Mark smiled, and put Cathy back down on the ground. He stooped low to look in her face and wipe her tears.

'What happened?' he asked gently.

'We lost a wheel half-way down the hill. It went out of control and it got smashed.' At the thought of it, Cathy began to cry again.

Mark took her in his arms and hugged her. 'Now, now! If the Flippin' Flyer is broken, I'll fix it!'

Cathy pushed back from him quickly. 'Will yeh, Mark?

Will yeh? Will yeh, really?'

'Sure I will, no problem, chicken,' Mark assured her.

She took him by the hand and began to drag him towards the front door.

'Come on, Mark, I'll show yeh,' she said excitedly.

Mark went with her, down the stairs to the bottom floor. Beneath the stairwell was some storage space. There was a small odd-shaped door that led into it. Cathy opened the door and quickly disappeared inside. Mark could hear her grunting, then she emerged dragging a sack which she laid on its side, then grabbed the ends and tipped out the contents.

'Holy Jesus!' Mark exclaimed and began to rummage through the debris. All that remained of the Flippin' Flyer was firewood.

'What did yis hit? A bulldozer?' he asked.

'Can yeh fix it, Mark? Please,' Cathy begged.

Mark placed his hands on his hips. 'I suppose so. Give me a couple of days, I'll have it back right as rain.'

'A couple of days! But we can't wait a couple of days, Mark! The knock-out round is on Wednesday – that's the day after tomorrow. We have to go in that to get into the final on Saturday.'

'But, Cathy, I haven't got the time. It'll take – '

Cathy kicked the bundle of wood and went bounding up the stairs shouting back, 'Forget it, it doesn't matter.'

Mark felt terrible. He hadn't wanted to disappoint Cathy, but then he didn't want to make a promise he couldn't keep.

Chapter 6

THE CLICK FROM THE METALLIC SWITCHBOX reverberated throughout the factory. It took Mark more than an hour to clear away a corner of the factory where he could work on the project. Once the area was cleared, he then went to the huge design table and, removing the sheets of paper from his back pocket, clipped them under the bullclip of the reference board. His first task would be to draw templates of the designs he had drawn, to be copied three times. Wise & Co. always had hardboard sheets in stock specifically for this purpose. Mark manoeuvred the first hardboard sheet onto the design table and with yardstick, protractor and pencil began to lay down the first of the templates.

Some time later Mark heard the door bang closed in the distance. Then Sean McHugh's voice cried out, 'Mark! It's only me.'

'Down here, Mr McHugh, at the design table,' Mark called back wearily.

Mark was having trouble making the templates from his designs. He had already discarded one complete sheet of hardboard. Sean's shiny red face came into the light.

'How's it going?' he asked.

'Not great,' answered Mark. 'I can't get these fuckin' templates right.' Frustration was setting in.

From his inside pocket Sean took a metal spectacle case from which he unfolded a very old pair of glasses. He put them on, clipped the box shut and inserted it back in his pocket. He was looking at the designs as he began to remove his coat.

'Right, then. Let's have a look at these,' he said.

Mark smiled and gladly stood aside for the older man, who was full of confidence. Suddenly Mark felt a little less lonely. Sean pointed at the designs with a pencil.

'This bow-back top spar here – you'll hardly have time to do a bentwood back spar for all three of them.' Sean looked over the rim of his glasses at Mark, tilting his head forward.

Mark had his answer ready. 'No I wouldn't. So I was goin' to cut it out of the half-inch plywood. I was goin' to cut six on the flat and nail two together for each back.' He traced the design with his finger on the dust that lay on the design table.

Slowly Sean McHugh smiled. 'Clever little bastard, aren't yeh?' he said, with a hint of admiration in his voice.

Mark laughed.

'Mind you – these suites won't last pissing time,' Sean added.

'They're not supposed to,' Mark replied, and both men smiled.

Sean snapped open his yardstick, ready to go to work. 'Right, son. You make us a cup of tea and I'll get working on these templates.' Sean took the pencil from his ear and watched Mark walk away towards the canteen.

A couple of hours later Sean McHugh was on his third

mug of tea. He had already successfully drawn four sheets of templates which Mark was now cutting on the bandsaw. It was already midnight. Sean was running the pencil down along the yardstick when the problem dawned on him. He stopped abruptly. He took the designs from the bullclip and walked over to the bandsaw where Mark was working. Mark saw him coming and pressed the stop button on the saw. When the saw died into silence, Sean said, 'We have a problem, Mark.'

'What?' Mark asked, with a puzzled look on his face.

Sean laid the designs down on the bandsaw plate. He pointed to one of the drawings of the finished suites.

'These backs,' he began.

'What about them?' Mark asked.

'There'll be thirty-six panels and eighteen buttons in each back.'

'That's right.'

'And the seat cushions – there'll be nine panels, four buttons in each cushion, is that right?'

Mark studied the designs, then looked up at Sean. 'Yeh, that's right. It's all there on the design. What's the problem?'

Sean looked at Mark over the rim of his glasses, then slowly he removed them.

'Who's going to do the sewing?' he asked slowly.

Mark closed his eyes. 'Fuck – the sewing! Fuck!'

It was 1am and cold. Mark stood outside the door of 32 Gardiner Row. The ground-floor flat was in darkness, as it had been for the ten minutes he'd been standing there. Mark had left Sean cutting out the remainder of the templates for the framework and had set off hoping to solve the sewing problem. At last he plucked up the courage and rapped on the door. Nothing stirred inside the flat. He rapped again, this time harder. There was some movement from the far side of the door and he heard the hushed tones of voices. Finally the door opened and there stood Betty Collins, wrapped in a blanket.

'Mark Browne? What the fuck do you want this hour of the mornin'?'

She obviously had gone to bed with her hair tied up, though there were now strands of hair sticking out and hanging down in all directions. She wore no make-up and she looked more than a little groggy. But no matter, at that moment to Mark Browne she was a vision of beauty!

'I ... I have a problem, Betty,' he managed to get out.

'Let me guess! The turn-ups on your trousers fell down. Well, we only handle complaints between nine and five. Now fuck off!' She began to close the door.

Mark quickly put his hand against it. 'Betty, please. Just listen,' he implored.

As simply as he could, Mark gave Betty a synopsis of the situation. She stood listening for twenty minutes, wrapped in the blanket and shaking a little from the chill.

'... and so I need somebody who can sew. I thought of you.' Mark finished. He didn't mention, although he wanted to, that for the last forty-eight hours he'd done a lot of thinking about her.

Betty had listened to the whole story without interruption. When Mark had finished, she glanced over her shoulder then back to him, and said, 'I have to get dressed – and collect some things. You wait here. I'll just be a couple of minutes.'

True to her word, it was just a couple of minutes before Betty arrived out dressed, wrapped in a duffel coat, with her hair now freshly brushed. She had collected her scissors and measuring tape. The two of them walked to Wise & Co. in virtual silence.

By 5.15am Agnes Browne was up and on her way to the fruit wholesale markets, though her thoughts were with her eldest boy.

Meanwhile back in Wise & Co. Mark had completed the frames for the six single-seater chairs for the suites, and was nearly finished the first of the three-seater frames. After a short introduction to Sean McHugh, Betty had rolled up her sleeves and buried herself in the task of cutting out the patterns.

'I'm finished!' she announced just as Sean arrived with two mugs of tea, one for her and one for himself. He didn't bring one for Mark, because Mark wasn't a tea man, so to speak.

'Good girl yourself!' said Sean as he handed her the mug.

Cupping the mug in her hands and looking over the rim at Mark, she said to Sean, 'Jesus, he can work can't he!'

Sean nodded. 'Aye. Like no-one I've ever seen – and I've seen a few hammers being swung in this place over the years. He's an exceptional young man.' This was said in admiration, like that of a father for a son. Mark Browne had this effect on older men. Betty turned her thoughts back to her task.

'Mr McHugh, I need to get all this stuff back up to the flat to the machine. I'll never be able to carry it.'

'That's okay, love. We can load it into the van and I'll drive you up. Will it take long to run it up?'

'Nah! A little more than an hour.'

'I'll wait with yeh so, if that's all right?'

'Yeh sure, no problem, Mr McHugh. We better get goin'.'

They began to gather up the material, and had the van loaded in a couple of minutes. Sean called to Mark. 'Mark! We're taking this stuff up to the sewing machine. We should be back in just over an hour.'

Mark did not look up, not even the rhythm of his hammer swing was disturbed. He just called out, 'Okay, Mr McHugh,' and with the beads of perspiration popping out, even on his forearms, he worked on.

Forty-five minutes later Mark had the final frame completed and the webbing fixed to all nine frames. He was tired. It would be half an hour before Sean returned with Betty. He wiped his brow and strolled to the design table, sat up on the high stool and with Sean's pencil began doodling on a blank sheet of paper. Like all soldiers when there's a lull in the battle, fear starts to creep in.. As he doodled his mind wandered to Greg Smyth and Frank Reel,. who were sleeping soundly in the Gresham hotel. What if he was wasting his time? What if they didn't go for the deal? What if they wouldn't even come down to the factory and look? Where would he get the fifty pounds to pay his Mammy back?

If Sean McHugh was right, unless he could convince Smyth and Reel to carry on doing business with Wise & Co., soon there would be no Wise & Co. and he would have no job. He shook his head vigorously to dispel these thoughts, and as he did he looked at what he had been doodling on the blank sheet of paper and laughed to himself. He took the piece of paper and gathering up what was left of the plywood and deal he carried the lot down to the bandsaw and began working again.

Just over forty minutes later he had replicated his doodle in wood and was writing on it with a permanent ink marker when Sean McHugh's van pulled up outside the door. Mark smiled to himself and looked up at the clock. It was 6.20am.

By 7.15 the work was done! The three stood appraising their night's labour.

'You've done a fine job, Mark! A really fine job,' Sean said, now a little refreshed having had an hour's sleep in an armchair in Betty Collins's flat. Mark stood with his arms folded. Betty reached over and laid her hand on his forearm.

'They're beautiful!' she exclaimed.

It was her hand touching his arm that excited Mark more than the praise she gave his work.

'Right!' said Mark. 'It's time to get these two fellows down to have a look!'

'Are you going straight up to the Gresham?' asked Sean.

'I have to go home first, clean up and change into me new outfit!' Mark turned to Betty. 'Betty, thanks very much – I really couldn't have done it without yeh. Make up a bill for whatever it is and I'll pay yeh.'

Betty gave a short laugh. 'Mark Browne! Let me tell yeh two things! Firstly, there is no bill – it was nice to be doin' somethin' different, I really enjoyed it. Secondly, if you think I'm leavin' here before findin' out what those men think of our work, you've another think comin' to yeh. Go get them, I'll be here when yeh get back!'

Mark smiled and headed off down the factory. Sean called to him. 'Mark – the door is this way,' and he pointed in the opposite direction.

Mark laughed. 'Yeh, I know, Mr McHugh! I just have to collect somethin' to bring home.'

As Mark vanished around the corner toward the band-saw, Sean put his arm around Betty's shoulder and took her into the canteen for an early-morning cup of tea.

Mark struggled in the door of the flat. The object was heavier than he had expected and he was tired from carrying it all the way up from Wise & Co. under his arm. It was also awkward so he tried to manoeuvre it through the doorway with as little noise as possible. Everyone was asleep and Agnes had long since gone to work. He left it on the floor in the kitchen. Mark quickly changed out of his overalls, washed and dressed himself up once again in his new clothes. No more than fifteen minutes had elapsed since the time he entered the flat. He was now back on the street, heading for the Gresham.

At 8.15am precisely, Mark walked up the marble steps of the Gresham hotel. At that same time Cathy Browne was back home shrieking with delight and dancing around, for she had just discovered a brand new box cart in the middle of the kitchen floor with the legend 'Flippin' Flyer II' drawn on the side of it.

Mark found Greg Smyth and Frank Reel in the restaurant having breakfast. They were surprised to see him. But Greg stood and extended his hand. 'Good morning, son,' he exclaimed. He used the word 'son' because he had forgotten Mark's name.

Frank Reel rose too but he remembered. 'Mark, how are you? What brings you here this morning?' he asked as he shook hands warmly with Mark.

Mark liked the younger man and from the warmth of the handshake it was clear the feeling was mutual. The two men sat and Mark addressed Greg.

'I don't know what time you have planned to leave Dublin today, Mr Smyth, but I hope you have time to come and look at somethin' in the factory.'

'What is it?' Greg asked.

'Furniture, Mr Smyth.'

Greg Smyth put his hand over his eyes as if slightly in pain. 'Look, Mark, I never had a problem with the quality of Wise & Co.'s furniture. I think you're missing the point here. I really don't think there is anything you can show me that will change our mind.' It was obvious that he wasn't budging.

Frank Reel looked disappointed, but obviously knew enough not to intervene. The boss is always the boss.

Mark's voice was very calm, although inside he was starting to panic. 'Look, Mr Smyth, Mr Wise is a good and decent man and he has being doin' business with you for thirty years and from what you say he's never let you down. The least you owe us is fifteen minutes. What about it?'

Greg exhaled loudly.

Frank suddenly came to life. 'Mr Smyth, it's on the way to the airport, we could stop off there in the taxi,' he suggested.

After a tense couple of moments, Greg succumbed. 'Okay,' he said, and threw his serviette onto his plate.

'I'll wait outside until you're finished,' Mark said.

Frank stood up. 'That's okay, were finished anyway, aren't we, Mr Smyth?'

Of the twenty staff that were still employed in Wise & Co., twelve were young apprentices. The other eight were made up of Sean McHugh, a designer and six craftsmen.

The youngest of those eight was thirty-five years of age, the next youngest to him fifty-eight and the rest were all over sixty. When they had arrived for work that morning Sean McHugh had ushered them all into the canteen and when everyone had a mug of tea in his hand Sean began to tell them what was happening at Wise & Co. He informed them about the rapid drop in business. He told them of Mr Wise's declining health. He gave them the details of the previous day's meeting with Smyth & Blythe and finally he outlined Mark Browne's efforts to rescue the company. They listened in silence. When he had finished, Sean led the lot of them like a Japanese tour group out to the three suites, which they examined closely. They sat on the chairs. They turned them upside-down. One of the craftsmen even lay on the couch, deciding to judge it as most people judge their couch – by how comfortable it is to lie on and watch TV.

Suddenly Betty Collins let out a cry from the office. 'Mr McHugh – they're here in a taxi.'

For some reason, inexplicable to himself, Sean McHugh cried, 'They're here – everybody hide!'

Even more inexplicable was the fact that everybody did. Bodies scurried in all directions. Sean ran into the office and closed the door, then suddenly realised that he was the boss. He buttoned his collar, coughed and marched out to meet the customer, whispering from the side of his mouth to Betty Collins to 'Keep down.'

The first thing Mark noticed as he led the two men into the factory was how quiet it was. Nobody was working, the place looked like a ghost town. As he walked towards the corner where the three suites were, he looked around the factory and could feel pairs of eyes peering at him from the most unusual places. He scratched his head in wonderment but carried on none the less.

'Here yeh are,' Mark announced, and waved his hand across the three suites.

Frank Reel smiled. Greg Smyth said nothing, his face expressionless, and for a moment he didn't budge. Suddenly he moved into action. He was like a doctor examining a newborn baby. He turned the suites upside-down, he laid them on their sides, he sat in them and even stood on one of the armchairs. Mark watched nervously with his arms crossed. Sean moved to his side and put his hand on Mark's shoulder. Mark looked at him, worried. Sean simply winked.

Mark went over to the suites and stood face-to-face with Greg. 'Well, what do you think?' he asked.

Greg was holding one of the seat cushions and pulling roughly on the button to see would it come out.

'How much?' he asked simply.

Mark looked over Greg Smyth's shoulder at Sean, who promptly held up seven fingers. Mark took this to mean seventy pounds, but he wasn't a market dealer's son for nothing. 'Ninety pounds a suite,' Mark said evenly.

Sean put his hands up to his face.

'No! I wouldn't pay any more than eighty,' Greg Smyth answered very off-hand.

Mark extended his hand and simply said, 'Done!'

Greg Smyth took Mark's hand, smiled and turned to Sean. 'I'll take as many of these as you can make, Sean.'

Suddenly the empty factory erupted with cheers, and bodies rushed from every corner. Mark emitted a couple of short bursts of nervous laughter which turned into hearty laughter as the older craftsmen gathered around him, patting him on the back. Then he glanced towards Sean's office and saw Betty Collins standing at the doorway. Her eyes were watery. She was tired, but her smile was nearly the width of the doorway. Mark returned the smile, then raised his fist in the air and exclaimed, 'Yes!'

Chapter 7

LONDON

MANNY WISE LIKED TO DO THIS. Having just stepped from the shower in his beautiful apartment on the Edgeware Road he now sat naked on his leather office desk, a King Edward cigar in his left hand and a glass of Scotch and ice in his right. He sat entranced, with a smug smile on his face as if he were taking in some important programme on the television. This wasn't the case, however. Manny had opened his safe door and he now sat staring at the piles of money that lined the compartment. The Amsterdam connection had proved to be a winner. With the constant cheap supply of cocaine and heroin, Manny had set himself up with a nice little network of sales. He had four bars, one in Camden Town, one in Leytonstone, and two in Willesden that served as very profitable sales points for his merchandise. He also had about a dozen young boys, most of them runaways or homeless boys from Ireland, who had got off the boat in Liverpool ready to dig for gold in the streets, and as always happens very quickly found themselves homeless and penniless and most were glad to trade in the 'white death' for a taste of the good life. Unfortunately most of the salesmen became users and what they made – instead of going into bettering their lives – went straight up their nose or into their arm. Manny Wise cared not one iota about this. His bottom line was profit, regardless of the cost in human misery. The only human being Manny Wise cared about was Manny Wise.

Manny stood and walked back into the bathroom. The full-length mirror there didn't flatter him at all; his arse was beginning to spread and when he turned sideways he looked as if he was in the later stages of pregnancy. He moved from the bathroom back to the drinks cabinet and dropped some ice into his glass, over which he poured yet another Scotch. He then walked to the window and looked down on the Edgeware Road.

The unmarked police car was there where it always was, right across the road outside the Chinese restaurant. The police officer in the passenger seat looked up at the window. Manny quickly whipped the curtain back and wiggled his penis at the officer, giving him a big smile. He enjoyed taunting the police. Manny Wise was now one of the Big Boys, no longer a pawn in the game. He was now a big player and, he believed, untouchable. Manny's doorbell rang. He slipped on a silk boxer's robe, took a mouthful of Scotch and casually walked to the apartment door. The sight of the young man outside drew a smile from Manny.

'Joe!' he announced. 'You're looking great.' This was a lie. The young man standing at the door looked dreadful.

Thanks to his now developed drug habit, he had lost interest in his own appearance, and no longer washed, no longer worried about how he dressed. His cheeks were sunken and his teeth yellow from lack of nutrition, for Joe had long since stopped worrying about food too. Joe Fitzgerald, or whoever he was – for the young men that Manny recruited used more than one name as they moved about the city of London signing on for benefits – was one of Manny's runners.

Manny knew the boy as Joe Fitzgerald. He had met him in Liverpool Street station, a great recruiting spot for young derelicts. It had taken Manny just a cup of coffee and a five-pound note to lure what was once just a young petty criminal into the world of big drugs business. Although Joe was a likeable young man, Manny wouldn't trust him as far as he could throw him, in fact at this moment in time Manny had no-one he could trust. He often bemoaned this, as he believed that every arch criminal, or as he would describe himself, 'big business-man', should have a right-hand man. Manny had yet to find one, although he reasoned that anyone who would be good enough to be Manny Wise's right-hand man would hardly be found sleeping in a cardboard box or starving in Liverpool Street station.

With the cigar stuck in the side of his mouth Manny instructed the young boy to wait in the hallway.

'I have a couple of little packages for you. One to go to Leytonstone and one down to Camden Town.'

'Sure, Manny, sure.' The young man was shaking and his eyes danced in his head. 'The Old Bill are parked across the road, Manny,' he added.

'Don't you worry about the Old Bill, my son. You just

worry about getting your fuckin' arse to Camden and Leytonstone.'

The young man dropped his head and quietly said, 'Okay.'

Manny returned to his study and rummaged in the safe, lifting out two tinfoil packages neatly double wrapped in cellophane. As he lifted the packages from the safe, he noticed the now-yellowing envelope that read 'Dublin Papers', and he smiled to himself as he closed the safe door and spun the combination lock. As young Joe Fitzgerald left the building by the back entrance, Manny was already sitting feet up at the television, finishing his Scotch and scratching his scrotum.

Chapter 8

DUBLIN

THE CLINCHING OF THE SMYTH & BLYTHE order was just the beginning of a few weeks of intense work for Mark. All but a quarter of the factory had to be modified to suit the new formula of cut, assemble and cover. The other apprentices at Wise & Co. were a great help, as most of them were learning about this new system in college. The older tradesmen, however, withdrew to the remaining quarter of the factory space where they continued to turn out classic hardwood furniture.

Mark was consistently in the top five percent in his woodwork class. In the beginning of his second year in college he had decided to take another course, business studies. This delighted Agnes, as she now felt that not only would the Browne family turn out a tradesman but also a businessman. Mark was a natural at the business studies and in his first year he excelled. His teachers put it down to study, but Mark knew it was down to his mother's pedigree in street trading. So, as well as modifying the factory to cope with the target he had set of a hundred suites per month, Mark also needed to modify Wise & Co.'s business slightly.

He discussed this at length with Mr Wise and Sean McHugh, expressing his opinion that, were the soft furnishings side of the company to trade under a different name and as a different company to Wise & Co., then the hard furniture section could carry on, even in a modified way, without being 'tainted' by the image of cheap furniture. Both men agreed, and Mr Wise was particularly proud of Mark for making the effort to maintain the name of Wise & Co. and to associate it only with quality furniture. He insisted that since Mark had 'taken the ball' he should now run with it himself, and he told Mark he would leave it to him to organise and arrange this new company in his name. Benjamin Wise knew exactly what he was doing – he was grooming the young man so that he would be ready eventually to take over the entire business.

Mark contacted Michael Fox Jnr., the family solicitor. There were two contradictions here. Firstly, although he continued to use the 'Junior', Michael Fox, in his mid-sixties, belied the title. Secondly, to refer to him as the

Browne family solicitor was a bit of an exaggeration. The man had been used on only one occasion by the Brownes and that was when Simon went to court for playing football in the street. But he was the only solicitor Mark knew. Mark wished to form a new company specifically for the soft-furnishing side of Wise & Co.'s business. This presented little problem to Mr Fox, the only slight hiccup that arose was when Mr Fox asked Mark what he wished the company to be called. After a few moments' thought, Mark said, 'Senga Soft Furnishings Limited', and smiled contentedly to himself.

Later, Mr Wise was the only one to spot that the name was 'Agnes' backwards, which, Mark said, was no reflection on his mother's personality!

Little was seen of Mark in James Larkin Court over that few weeks as he worked night and day to hammer the factory into a routine where a hundred suites a month would be no problem. Mark had also partitioned off another section of the factory floor where he had installed three second-hand Singer industrial sewing machines that Sean McHugh had purchased at a very reasonable price. Maggie Collins had not been too pleased when Betty told her that she intended to work in Wise & Co. as one of the three machinists. Mark had also convinced Sean to employ two cutters and three labourers, bringing Wise & Co.'s total staff up to twenty-six, the first rise in personnel the factory had seen in over fifteen years. Betty Collins was enthusiastic about the challenge and rose to it like a salmon to a mayfly. She worked long hours. Her bubbly personality kept everybody up, and, as a bonus for Betty, for the first time in her young life she was in love!

The absence of Mark from the home was a bit of a

downer for the kids. Cathy, although she pretended to be disappointed, was quite happy with finishing second in the downhill go-cart race. But when she had burst in that Saturday to announce the result, Mark had not been there. Dermot too was missing Mark's company and now spent more and more of his time roaming the shops of Dublin relieving them of their goods in some of the most ingenious of fashions. Rory felt he had nobody to turn to with his fear of coming home each night. Twice more he had been chased by gangs of skinheads and on the last occasion just barely escaped. He longed for the summer so that he could walk home in the daylight. Agnes had now extended Frankie's 'period' by another month, but made it very clear that this extension was a temporary reprieve, not a change of mind. Agnes's most pressing concern was young Simon. Following her decision on Frankie, Simon saw the opportunity for him too to depart school and get a job. This didn't go down well with Agnes at all. Frankie, she explained to Simon, was being thrown out of school, where the teacher had described Simon as a slow but lovable pupil. Nevertheless, Simon stuck to his guns and had now fixed himself up with an appointment for an interview for a job as a porter in St Patrick's hospital.

Having just broken this news to Agnes, Simon sat awaiting her pronouncement on it.

'So yeh've got yourself an interview?' Agnes asked.

'Ye ... ye ... ye ... yes, Ma ... Ma ... Mammy,' Simon tried to be as firm as he could.

'D'yeh realise what an interview means?'

Simon looked at his mother blankly, not really understanding the question.

'The man ...' she began slowly, 'will ask you questions.'

Simon's brow rose, his mouth hung open and he slowly nodded his head.

'And you will have to answer them – speak to him.'

'Su ... su ... so?'

Agnes leaned over and placed her hand on Simon's hand. 'You have a stutter, luv,' Agnes exclaimed, as if it were going to be a surprise to Simon.

'Su ... su ... su ... so?'

Agnes was trying to be as gentle as she could. 'Do you not feel a stutter might affect your chances of gettin' the job?'

'Na ... na ... no, wa ... why should it?' Simon asked, quite genuinely not seeing a problem.

Agnes exhaled. 'Jesus, son. If someone needs a bedpan and calls you, by the time you say wa ... wa ... wa ... what d'yeh want, they'll have shit in the bed!'

'Mm ... Mm ... Ma! ... I'm a p ... p ... porter, not a bl ... bleedin' nu ... nu ... nurse.'

Agnes had to acknowledge the boy's resolve. 'All right. Of course I wish you well, I'm just afraid of yeh being disappointed, that's all. If you get the job yeh can take it.'

The boy smiled and hugged his mother. 'D ... d ... don't worry, Mam. I ... I'll get the job!' Simon declared confidently.

Ten days later Simon was standing in the toilet just off the personnel office of St Patrick's hospital. Outside in the waiting room there were twenty other hopefuls for the porter's job. Simon looked at himself in the mirror. With a hand each side of the sink he leaned close to his reflection and inhaled deeply.

'How ... now ... brown ... ca ... ca ... cow!' he said to his reflection. Once again he inhaled deeply. 'Around the rugged rock the ra ... ra ... ragged ra ... ra ... rascal ra ... ra ... ah, fuck it!'

Behind him in a cubical the toilet flushed, the door opened and out strode a young man, maybe a year or two older than Simon. The fellow walked straight to the exit door, opened it, then turned to Simon, paused for a moment, and said, 'Fuck me! I can see I'm up against it!' He laughed as he exited.

Simon's heart sank. He returned to the waiting room and sat down. Each time he caught the eye of the young man Simon would blush a little. He fixed his gaze on the door of the personnel manager's office and waited.

The door opened and yet another young applicant left the room. This one looked a little dejected. Simon chastised himself for feeling glad at the applicant's expression. The secretary entered the office and closed the door. She had brought in a new batch of applications. Minutes later she opened the door again and called, 'Mr Simon Browne, please.'

Simon had been quite calm up to that – bordering on confident. He couldn't explain what happened the minute he heard that young lady call his name. His legs turned to jelly, his stomach went queasy and he felt light-headed. He suddenly found himself closing the office door from the inside without remembering how he had got up and walked to the door at all. The room was sparsely decorated. There were four filing cabinets, dark green in colour, and beside them was a table stacked up with even more files. There was a huge map on one wall which took in counties Dublin, Kildare, Wicklow, Louth and Meath. The title on the map read Eastern Health Board Area. In the centre of the room was a well-worn dark brown wooden desk behind which sat a rather gaunt-looking man, wearing thick black-rimmed glasses. He had on a navy suit, blue shirt and tie, and had a head that refused to believe it was bald, with a thick growth of hair on each side and what looked like twenty banjo strings across the top. Without speaking, the man indicated a chair on the opposite side of the desk on which Simon promptly sat down. He remained quiet for a couple of moments while the man read the application form he held in his hands. Simon recognised his own writing on the back page. The bald man gently placed the application form on the desk in front of him, looked up at Simon and began.

'Su ... su ... so ... yo ... yo ... you are Si ... Si ... Simon Ba ... Ba ... Browne.'

For a moment Simon was stunned. He slowly nodded his head in assent.

The man went on. 'Su ... su ... so, wa ... wa ... why do you want to leave sa ... sa ... school, Si ... Simon?'

For the first time Simon spoke. 'I wa ... want ta ... to wo ... work, and eh, an ... anyway mi ... my teacher sa ... sa ... says I'm a sl ... sl ... slow pupil.'

Simon started work as the new trainee porter in St Patrick's hospital the following Monday.

* * *

That same week Agnes received a letter from her sister Dolly. Before even going on to tell Agnes of her latest complaint – a constant headache which she suspected was a brain tumour – Dolly expressed great delight that Agnes would be coming on a visit with young Trevor; and although Agnes had told Dolly in her letter of her bingo win, the two crisp $20 bills accompanied Dolly's letter yet again. Within hours of receiving the letter Agnes set off to book her flights.

Constellation Travel in Liffey Street was owned and run by the Donegan brothers, Joe and Tim. Along with the two men, bachelors and in their fifties, the company had only one other employee and that was Margaret Sharp, who did secretarial work for the men. On the day Agnes arrived at the office, Margaret was out sick and Joe was delivering tickets to a client across town. Tim was a little disgruntled – dealing with members of the public was not his forte, and he dreaded being left to mind the store. Tim was on the 'phone when Agnes entered the office. He indicated as much to her and he hoped by the time he was finished his call that Joe would have returned. In the meantime, Agnes browsed through a couple of brochures, speaking the names of the destinations aloud.

'Mag–a–loof. Jesus!' She picked up another brochure. 'Santa–pooz–na. Mother of God!'

Tim was now standing at the counter and by way of opening the conversation, he said to Agnes, 'Well, Madam, fancy a trip to the sun?' He smiled.

Agnes spun around to face him. 'Oh God no, luv! I'd never go anywhere I couldn't pronounce.'

'Well then, what can I do for you?' Tim suspected this lady was here to enquire about a trip to Lourdes. Another miracle-chaser, he thought.

Agnes placed her handbag on the counter and smiled at the man. 'I want to go to Canada.'

Tim returned the smile. He took a pad and pencil and began to make notes. 'Right, Canada. And where in Canada?'

'Me sister's.'

Tim looked up from the pad. The lady was still smiling, so this obviously wasn't a joke. He tried again.

'And where does your sister live?'

'I told yeh – in Canada.'

'Yes, but whereabouts in Canada?'

'Oh sorry, luv.' Agnes began to root in her handbag and extracted Dolly's letter. She read the address aloud. '1202 Ironwood Court.'

Tim nodded at the lady slowly in a silent gesture for her to go on with the rest of the address but she didn't, she just looked again and smiled.

'And where is Ironwood Court?'

Agnes was now getting towards the end of her tether. 'In fuckin' Canada.'

Tim made a gentle tug at the letter. Agnes hung on.

'May I have a look at the address, please?' he asked, exasperated.

Reluctantly Agnes let him have the letter, but folded it in half before handing it over so he couldn't read the whole page.

Tim said aloud. 'Ah! I see – in *Toronto* in Canada.'

Agnes nodded her head. 'Good man.'

Tim bent under the counter to get himself a fare-and-route manual. He placed the huge book on the counter and began flicking through the pages. He eventually stopped at a page and ran his finger down a column.

'Right, then. You could go by Geneva.' He looked up.

Agnes thought for a moment. 'Geneva? Is that like a jumbo?'

'No, Geneva is in Switzerland.'

'I want to go to Can-a-da for God's sake.'

'You will be going to Canada – but if I send you through

Geneva it would be the most cost-effective way.'

'But I'll get to me sister's?'

Tim smiled a broad smile. He wished this woman would just disappear. 'You will of course, madam. Have you decided on a date yet?'

'No, not yet.'

'Ah! So, really, you're just looking for the fare?'

'No, no, I have the fare, I just need to know the price.'

'I can get you a charter price of £199 return – that's really good value, believe me.'

'That sounds grand. Yeh, that's for me. I'll be bringing me son as well, he's dying to meet his new uncle. He's a Canadian, yeh know, bank manager.'

'And how old is he?'

'About forty-one, I think. Let me see ...'

'Your son is forty-one?'

'No! His uncle is forty-one. Me son is only eight.'

Tim Donegan had had enough. 'Well, once he's below twelve he'll get a fifty percent reduction. That's half price. So, there you have it. When you have a date, drop in and see us and we'll look after you.'

'What's your name, luv'.

'My name? Eh Tim, Tim Donegan.'

'Grand, Tim, I'll ask for you the next time I come in, because I couldn't go through all them questions again.'

Agnes smiled, gathered her bag and left the travel agent's office. As soon as she was gone Tim Donegan put on the kettle for a hot cup of tea and took a valium.

Chapter 9

FRANKIE BROWNE SAT ON THE SMALL two-foot wall that surrounded St Jarlath's church. Beside him, down behind the wall, three other skinheads were playing poker. Although a keen poker player himself, Frankie didn't want to join the boys in their game today, his mind was elsewhere. He had just ten days of his mother's deadline left and still had nowhere to go. He had no intention of getting a job. Jobs were for 'mugs'. He was no mug; he was too smart to be a mug. He thought about going to London – he had heard London was a great town for scams. Bunty Flynn said his brother was in London for three years and was signing on the dole at six different offices, making nearly £200 a week. That's the kind of money Frankie was interested in, real money. He took a last drag on the cigarette and flicked the butt towards the curb. Just then from around the side of St Jarlath's church another skinhead, 'Copper' Cullen, came running. He was breathless by the time he reached the group.

Frankie stood up. 'What's up, Copper?'

'The lads – the lads have a queer cornered up Peck's Lane. Come on!'

The card game was abandoned and the five of them

took off around the side of the church. Peck's Lane was just a minute's run from where they had been. As they came to the entrance of the lane they could see six of their skinhead friends milling around a slumped figure. Because the figure was now on the ground the gang resigned themselves to just booting the young man.

Frankie was the last of the five to join the attacking gang. As he arrived into the group he saw a gap in their legs and rammed his boot through the space straight into the back of the figure. This elicited a sharp yelp from the young man and a whoop of joy from Frankie. Some of the others stood back to let Frankie have a good go. As he stood over the body he could see clearly that the left arm was broken, with the wrist bent backwards, the head was matted with blood, and what had probably been fairly decent clothes were now in tatters. He picked the back of the victim's neck for his next target and drew his boot back. As he did so the body whimpered. For a moment Frankie hesitated – there was something about that whimper. It was babyish, and he recognised it! He had heard it before years ago. He had heard it just after his father had died and he and the other Browne boys still shared one bed. He leaned down, took the shoulder of the body, and turned it towards him to see the battered face of a barely conscious Rory Browne. Before he passed out, Rory said simply, 'Frankie?'

* * *

'So what do you think?' Mark asked, unsure that he had done the right thing.

The two older men didn't reply. They continued to walk around the dusty shop, glancing at the ceiling, stomping their feet on the floor. Mark looked at Betty. She was linking his arm. She gave him a little squeeze and smiled.

'The rent is only £80 a month and we can do most of the fitting ourselves,' Mark went on.

Still there was no reply from either Sean McHugh or Benjamin Wise. Sean had both hands thrust into his pockets, and Mr Wise had a hand up each opposite sleeve and looked as if he was wearing a muff. Eventually Mr Wise spoke.

'Eighty pounds a month?'

'Yeh, eighty pounds a month.'

Mr Wise turned to Sean. 'That's not bad, Sean, is it?'

'Not bad at all, Mr Wise. Not bad at all.'

Mark moved from Betty's side towards the two men and as he did he said, 'It'll give us our own retail outlet – just for the class furniture, the hardwood stuff.'

'And you're going to call it what? Tell me again, Mark.'

Mark spoke loudly and boldly. 'Wise & Co. Bespoke Furniture.'

Again Mr Wise turned to Sean and spoke to him as loudly as Mark had spoken. 'Bespoke Furniture, Sean! I like that. What do you think?'

Sean smiled. 'I think it's a great idea, Mr Wise. You and me run the shop, leave the factory stuff to Mark.'

Mr Wise did not reply. Instead, he looked at Mark, standing there, tall, broad and handsome. He envied the boy his youth and his energy. Of course it was a great idea. The young man waited expectantly. Mr Wise removed his hands from his sleeves and extended his arms sideways, pushing his palms in the air as if he were making an offering. 'Well, young Mark Browne, it looks like we've got ourselves a shop!'

Mark smiled broadly and now launched into his plans for the shop, taking Mr Wise by the arm and showing him each of his ideas for the layout, inch by inch. Mark was in full flight when a rapping at the front door stopped his gallop. All three men turned to see young Tom Lewis, an apprentice from the soft furnishing side of the business, standing breathless at the front door, pointing to the lock and mouthing the words, 'Open the door.'

It was Betty who opened it. Tom pushed straight past her to Mark's side. 'Mark, your Mammy's been on the 'phone to the factory. You've to go down to St Patrick's hospital, your brother's had an accident.'

Mark paled. 'Which brother? Did she say which brother?'

'Rory – she said it was Rory.'

Without another word to the elderly gentlemen or to Betty, Mark left what was to be Wise & Co.'s new retail outlet like a bullet from a gun. He began to feel light-headed as his feet pounded towards St Patrick's general hospital.

By the time Mark arrived at the hospital Rory had been shifted from Casualty to Intensive Care. Confused, Mark walked the corridors as quickly as he could trying to find Intensive Care, and luckily he bumped into Simon. Simon was pushing a trolley, wearing the green housecoat of a hospital porter.

'Simon, what's happening?'

'Ja ... Ja ... Jesus, Ma ... Mark! He's rea ... really bad.'

Mark was anguished. 'Oh no! Where's Intensive Care?'

'Co ... co ... come on, I'll show you.'

Just a couple of minutes later Mark was standing by the

bedside of his younger brother Rory, along with his mother, Dermo, Cathy, Simon and little Trevor. Rory looked dreadful. Both his eyes were puffed up, and were black and closed.

Agnes told Mark the full extent of the damage. 'His nose is broken, and his left arm. He has three fractured ribs.' She sobbed heavily between sentences. 'He has stitches under his left eye and over his right eye, as well as fourteen stitches in his back. They could have killed him.' Agnes began to cry uncontrollably.

Mark took her in his arms and held her tightly. He spoke gently into her ear. 'Mammy, he's okay now, he's safe. You're just upsetting the kids.'

'I know, I'm sorry, luv. I just can't believe it!'

'Shush! It's okay, Ma, I'm here now. Look, you take Trevor home and start the dinner, and we'll be along shortly after yeh. Go on! He's okay now, he's fine.'

Agnes didn't reply, but held her handkerchief to her eyes and nodded her head. She went to Rory's bedside and gave him a gentle kiss on the cheek. Through swollen lips, Rory muttered, 'Thanks, Ma.'

'I'm going home to get the tea for the kids, I'll be back later luv, okay?'

'Okay, Ma.'

Agnes took Trevor and left the hospital. Mark sat on the edge of Rory's bed and leaned down closer to him. Rory looked up into Mark's face. Mark smiled and winked. Rory felt safe; he blinked and as he did two huge tears fell from his eyes.

'So, was it skinheads?' Mark asked.

Rory simply nodded.

'How many of them?'

'Eight or ten,' Rory mumbled.

'The bastards! In packs like wolves.' Mark was struggling to control his anger. He placed his hand gently on Rory's hand and held it firmly but not too tightly. 'Did you recognise them, Rory?'

Rory looked into Mark's eyes a little longer than he should have, then shook his head and mumbled, 'No.'

Mark slowly nodded his head and then turned to Dermot. 'Dermo, you bring Cathy with yeh and head for home. Tell Mammy I'll be along in a few minutes, I just want to talk to Rory on me own, okay?'

Dermot didn't want to go but acceded to his brother's wishes. 'Well, all right, but I know what youse two are goin' to talk about, Mark, and if you're goin' after them I want in on it. He's my brother as well, yeh know,' Dermot said as he picked up Cathy's coat.

Mark smiled and put his arm around Dermot's neck. He pulled him close in a mock strangulation. 'Okay, tough guy. Don't you worry, you'll be there.'

'I mean it,' Dermot insisted.

'I know you do and so do I, Dermo, I promise. Now go on off with yeh. Get Cathy out of here.'

When the two children had disappeared out the ward door Mark turned his attention again to Rory. 'You recognised them, didn't yeh, Rory?'

Rory did not reply, nor did he nod or shake his head, and his eyes started to fill up.

'Were they locals? From our area?'

Rory began to sob loudly, his body quivering as he gasped for breath.

Mark leaned down and hugged him. 'Shush! Take your time, take it easy. I'm not trying to upset yeh, I just want to know, that's all. Calm down.'

In a few moments Rory had calmed down and the crying had been reduced to sniffles. He gave a short cough to clear the phlegm that always accompanies sobbing. Mark leaned very close to him, took both his shoulders in his hands and spoke firmly but gently, all the time looking into Rory's eyes.

'Who was it?' Mark said it in a way that demanded an answer.

Rory's lips began to quiver and the answer trickled out. 'It was Frankie.'

Mark's grip tightened automatically and he actually hurt Rory, who gave a little groan. Mark's face, which had been pale, was now blue. He stood up quickly. 'I'll see yeh later, Rory.' Mark spun on his heel and left St Patrick's hospital, a dangerously angry young man.

Mark did not so much enter the flat as explode into it. He looked fit to kill. Cathy, Trevor and Simon were sitting on the sofa watching the television, and all three jumped simultaneously and sat gaping at the sight of this raving lunatic that resembled their brother. Mark moved swiftly to the kitchen area. Dermot had the frying pan on the cooker and was putting sausages onto it.

'Where's Frankie, Dermo?'

'Frankie? He's not here.' There was a tremor in Dermot's voice. Mark went to the bedroom. The first thing that caught his eye was the second drawer from the top in the chest of drawers, which was pulled out and empty. Mark yanked open the door of the wardrobe, and it too was empty – everything gone, including Mark's new businessman's outfit.

'The bastard!'

Mark returned to the kitchen. Dermot stood aghast, with a half a pound of Haffner's sausages hanging from his left hand like a giant pearl necklace. The other three children, equally shocked and not a little frightened, peered in from the TV room.

'Where's Mammy?' Mark asked Dermot.

'She's ... she's in her room ... her bedroom.'

Mark spun around and went to his mother's bedroom door. He rapped lightly but quickly and opened the door. Agnes was sitting on the bed. Her shoulders were slumped and she slowly turned her head around to Mark. She had been crying. Mark stood in the doorway.

'Are you all right, Mammy?'

Agnes didn't answer her eldest son. Instead, she lifted up her left hand. She was holding a suede boot. Slowly she turned the boot upside-down. It was empty.

At that moment the B&I ferry *Hibernia* was just passing the Kish, the last lighthouse ship on the Irish coast. The ferry was heading for England. So was Frankie Browne.

Chapter 10

THE WEEKS FOLLOWING FRANKIE'S DEPARTURE were difficult for Agnes. The situation had left the younger children bewildered and her eldest boy Mark a very angry young man. She tried to cope with Mark's anger while at the same time coming to terms with her own sadness at the loss of a son, black sheep or not. Naturally she was angry with Frankie, and yes she was bitterly disappointed that her Canada trip would now not take place. But her most overwhelming feeling was a kind of sadness that only a mother can know at the loss of a son. For that's how she perceived it, that she had indeed lost one of her precious boys, and in tragic circumstances. No amount of comforting from her friends who told her she was better off without him could lessen the impact of her loss. Her heart was scarred.

Mark burned his anger off by working harder, and redoubled his efforts at Wise & Co., and within two months had the new store open and trading. Within an hour of Wise & Co. Bespoke Furniture opening its doors it took its very first order. Mrs Patricia Kearney, wife of the good doctor Matthew Kearney of Seafield Road in Clontarf, placed an order for a reproduction Edwardian dining-room suite. Sean McHugh and Mr Wise fussed over the good lady like doting professors, although when she had left the store they giggled and clapped like little schoolboys.

'I thought I handled that very well, Sean, didn't you think so?' Mr Wise remarked, looking at himself in a dressing-table mirror and straightening the bright red bow-tie he now wore with his white shirt and navy blazer. He had decided that the shop owner should dress like a gentleman.

Sean was sitting at the bureau, writing Mrs Kearney's order into the order book, including in it the dimensions, size, and style of the unit. 'We should have done this years ago Mr Wise, we're naturals, born salesmen!'

'True, Sean, true. Do you know, Sean, I could sense what she wanted and it was just a case of steering her in the right direction.'

'Yes, well, we –' Sean began.

'Do you know, Sean, I've always had a way with women. I mean that of course in the nicest possible way,' Mr Wise interrupted Sean.

'Yeh! Sure, you're brilliant,' Sean said flatly.

Mr Wise was much too excited to notice Sean's annoyance at his constant use of the word 'I' instead of 'we', just then. But later, when Sean had gone up to the factory with the order slip to Mark, and as Mr Wise sat in the quiet shop alone, it dawned on him how in his excitement he had excluded his long-serving employee, and friend, from the celebrations of the sale. So he left the shop for fifteen minutes, and locked the door behind him, putting up a note saying 'back shortly'. He slipped into a shop just a couple of doors down from Wise & Co. Bespoke Furniture.

When Sean arrived back from the factory Mr Wise was dealing with a rather posh lady customer. She held a photograph in her hand and was trying with some difficulty to explain to Mr Wise exactly what she required. As Sean entered the store, the tiny bell on the door clanged. Mr Wise spun around, and with a very grandiose gesture he said to the lady, 'Ah now, Mrs Dolan, saved by the bell!'

The woman looked up at Sean over her half-moon glasses. Mr Wise walked her towards Sean.

'This is Mr Sean McHugh, the store manager. If anyone can help you it's Mr McHugh, isn't that right, Sean?'

Sean removed his brown derby hat in deference to the lady, and holding it against his chest with his left hand he half-bowed to her. 'What's the problem, madam?' Sean asked and immediately looked at Mr Wise, who smiled and winked at him.

The lady showed the photograph to Sean. He instantly recognised the piece of furniture in the black and white shot. 'This is a Louis XIV tallboy,' he pronounced.

'Yes it is!' the lady chirped, delighted that she was now speaking to an expert. 'I'm looking for the thingie that goes underneath.'

Sean nodded and smiled. 'Yes, indeed, that's called the maid's step, and that's really what it was – a step the maid would use to stand on when reaching for items on the tallboy. We can run you up one of these to match your unit in no more than ten days.'

The woman's face lit up. 'I have walked Dublin,' she said, 'in search of anyone who could even understand what I was talking about.' She was obviously thrilled.

Sean took her down to the order book where he did a

little pencil sketch of the piece, gave her a rough estimate of the price and she departed, very happy, and having left a deposit with the two men. As soon as she had gone Mr Wise exclaimed, 'Brilliant! You were absolutely brilliant, Sean. Boy, what a team we're going to make!'

Sean beamed, and reddened a little. 'Yes, I thought that went well, Mr Wise.'

'Well? You were fantastic! You had her eating out of your hand! Lucky you're married, Sean, or we should be facing serious female problems in this store!'

The two men laughed uproariously and Sean positively blushed this time. As the laughter faded, Sean sat down on his chair at the bureau and rested his elbow on a brown paper parcel. 'What's this?' he asked.

'Oh ... it's, em, something for you, Sean,' Mr Wise replied, very off-hand.

Sean picked up the parcel and slowly opened it to find two gleaming white shirts and a new red dicky-bow tie still in its box. He looked up slowly at his old friend. The words of thanks wouldn't come, but really they weren't necessary.

Mr Wise tried to brush it off as a business thing. 'Well, if you're going to be the store manager you should look like the store manager, wouldn't you agree?'

'Yes, Mr Wise, I do agree,' Sean said softly to his new-found team mate. 'But if I'm the store manager, what are you going to be?'

Mr Wise thought for just a moment, then replied, 'I shall be the managing director!'

The two men beamed at each other, and Sean trotted off to put on the kettle.

Never before had such a small store had only two staff

with such high-powered titles, Mark remarked that night, relating the story to Betty. For his part, Mark was enjoying his new role as factory manager. He had introduced a piece-work system in an effort to keep the output of the factory up. It worked well. Mark was also enjoying his newfound wealth, for his wage packet now contained £37 after deductions for tax and social welfare insurance payments. Of this he passed £10 on to Agnes, put £20 away in a savings account and easily managed on the £7 that was left. Life was going well for him and he would soon be making his first trip abroad to London to visit a potential new customer who had made some enquiries through Greg Smyth. He looked forward to this as it would be his first trip abroad – in fact, with the exception of his camping holiday in Blessington years ago, it would be his first trip outside Dublin! He now possessed two good suits, several white shirts and matching ties – all he needed now was a suitcase. Mark felt good.

The one tiny little cloud blocking his sunshine was how quiet and somewhat sad Agnes had been since Frankie's departure. But Mark could do little about this, especially since he was glad that Frankie was gone. He decided to leave the issue with his mother and hope she would come out of it herself.

And over the next few months there was plenty to lift Agnes's mind from thoughts of her second-eldest son overseas.

Firstly, in that February of 1971 Agnes had to cope with the change to decimalisation. Something that used to be two shillings now became ten pence. The sixpence was gone, so to was the thrupenny bit and the half-crown. In their place came the ½p, 1p, 2p, 5p, 10p, and 50p coins.

One pound was now the same as 100 new pennies, where before it had been two hundred and forty old pennies. The government guideline for the exchange rate was fairly simple: one new penny was worth two old pennies. Agnes thought this was fine, up to a point, but if one new penny equalled two old pennies and one hundred new pennies equalled one new pound, where previously it had been worth two hundred and forty pence, what happened to the missing forty pennies? Agnes suspected that the government kept them!

On top of trying to cope with decimalisation, Agnes was now trying to handle the upheaval of her new move. She'd been out a couple of times to the new house in Finglas. The journey took ages and the house seemed miles away. The bus took her past Glasnevin cemetery, even a dairy, through the tiny village of Finglas where the double-decker Number 40 bus had great difficulty in negotiating the narrow bridge that crossed the Fionnglas river from Finglas East to Finglas West where her new home was. Thankfully, once the bus reached its terminus on Barry Road, Agnes had just a one-minute walk to her new house on Wolfe Tone Grove.

Agnes still hated the thought of leaving Dublin's city centre. She had been born, christened, reared, confirmed, wooed, kissed and wed within a one-mile radius of James Larkin Court, and although all her furniture and personal things were carefully packed and ready for the move, Agnes knew that the memories encapsulated in that one-mile circle could not be taken out to the country. Her attitude to the move had softened just a little when that January two bombs had exploded in Dublin's city centre, a spin-off of the Northern troubles, and two people were killed in the bombings. Agnes's mother-hen instinct told her that the coop was now a little bit too close to danger and that her 'chicks' would be safer eight miles away in Finglas.

Even so, the Browne family did not depart 92 James Larkin Court until three days after everyone else had left the street. There had been a massive party a week previously in Foleys. Mr Foley had bought drink for everyone and supplied spare ribs free of charge. This was something Foley did from time to time as a kind of grand gesture – although there was method in his madness as the salty ribs made his clients drink even more.

Agnes sat in her usual corner, beside her the empty seat of her never-to-be-forgotten best friend Marion Monks, whose death had broken Agnes's heart three years ago. After a few bottles of cider Agnes began to talk to the empty chair. 'Ah Jaysus, Marion, listen to them! The music of The Jarro! Will we ever hear the likes of it again?'

The music to which Agnes referred could not be played on any instrument, but was the cackle of voices and rhythmic banter of the inner-city folk, the symphony of unanswered questions and impossible statements, that were so much of the colour of Dublin: 'Hey, Mr Foley. A vodka with ice – and fresh ice, none of that frozen stuff!' This would be followed by a howl of laughter.

'Where were yeh goin' yesterday when I saw yeh, goin' to work?'

'Where was I goin'? I was in a hurry.'

'I was thinkin', 'cause when I caught up with yeh, yeh were gone!'

These conversations would make perfect sense to the participants!

Pierre arrived into the party at around 2am with boxes full of pizzas which were promptly scoffed by all and sundry. Pierre's rendition of 'Poor Auld Dicey Reilly' in his thick French accent brought the house down. The party went on until the early hours of the morning, and strangely for a Dublin party died a quiet death. Then the hard men and women of Dublin city, not prone to great gestures of affection, merely nodded to each other and said 'Good luck' as they parted with old neighbours, in some cases never to see them again.

When the last bit of furniture was on the removals van outside 92 James Larkin Court and the back of the van was hammered up, Agnes sat into the front seat beside the driver with Trevor on her lap. The van shuddered to a start as the driver rammed it into first gear, and slowly made its way up the middle of the deserted James Larkin Court.

The last resident to leave the street was young Dermot Browne. He dashed after the van as it crept up the hill and climbed aboard, clutching under his arm the steel green-painted street sign which he had unscrewed from the wall. The sign was the property of Dublin Corporation – or had once been; it now belonged to Dermot Browne. In cream Gaelic letters it simply read: 'James Larkin Court, Dublin 1.'

The Browne family were the last to take up residence on the newly built street of Wolfe Tone Grove. There were forty-eight houses on the road, twenty-four each side, the even numbers on the right and the uneven numbers on the left. Agnes Browne and her children, in Number 43, were in the third last house on the left at the bottom of the street. Wolfe Tone Grove was on a slight hill, making

Agnes's end of the road slightly higher than the lower-numbered end of the road. Thus, although Agnes lived at the bottom of the road, because of the hill it eventually became known as the top of the road – only in Dublin! The terraced houses were built in blocks of six. Agnes's block ran from Numbers 37 to 47. Agnes knew from the moment she moved in that in her block alone she would have desperate trouble with her neighbours' names. They were, running from 37 upwards: the O'Donnells, the O'Connells, the McDonalds, the Brownes, the Bradys, and the Dowdalls. Cathy Browne and Cathy Dowdall were both thrilled that their new houses should be separated only by one garden. If the surnames were tricky, the children's names were too complex for Agnes to even ponder. Between the six families they had a total of forty-six children, and of these forty-six there were five Patricks, five Dermots, four Cathys, four Rorys, three Willies and three Jimmies.

The house had three bedrooms – well, two bedrooms and a box-room. Agnes took the box-room for herself. In the smaller of the two bedrooms she installed Cathy and Trevor, and in the larger room the four boys. Downstairs was a kitchen big enough to cook in but not to eat in, and the sitting-room cum dining-room. Behind the kitchen was a bathroom on one side of the small hallway and a toilet on the other side. The front garden was large enough at thirty feet by twenty-seven feet, the width of the house. The back garden was massive. Once again the width of the house, but this time over a hundred and twenty feet long.

Over the first few weeks all four older boys got stuck into working on the back garden with a variety of pick-axes and shovels, and over a period excavated a number of buckets, wheelbarrow-wheels and handles, and enough breeze blocks to build another home.

Agnes had put some money by to buy some new things for the house before the move, like new sheets and pillowcases for the beds. Mark supplied the suite of furniture for the sitting-room, which he bought at cost price from Senga Furnishings. It was a nice suite in mustard leatherette, one of the latest designs from Senga Furnishings which Mark called the 'Loretta' suite, again using his mother's second name. Agnes was very proud of this and never let the opportunity slip in any conversation to drop in the fact that she had a couch named after her. Agnes had purchased a bit of lino for the kitchen from 'Buddah' at the George's Hill Market. The gas cooker she had previously used in James Larkin Court had travelled well and now sat proudly beside the enamelled trough in the new kitchen. The largest and the most modern addition to the Browne's collection of furniture was provided as a 'moving in' gift by Pierre. Standing against a bare wall in the small kitchen like a monument, sat a gleaming white new Electrolux refrigerator. Having never had a refrigerator before, the Browne family were at a loss as to what to actually keep in it. Initially all they put there was butter and milk. Over a period of time it went on to contain bread, jars of jam, and even tins of processed peas. It was three months before Agnes realised it should be plugged in!

There was one open fire in the sitting-room and when lit this provided hot water for the entire family; Saturday bath nights now became a pleasure rather than a chore for Agnes.

There was no early bus from Finglas into Dublin city centre. The first bus left the terminus at five past six, much too late for Agnes or Carmel Dowdall to carry out their market business. Luckily, next door to Agnes in Number 45, lived the Bradys, Carol and her husband Ned. They had seven children and, needless to say, quickly became referred to as The Brady Bunch, although they couldn't have been more unlike The Brady Bunch had they tried, God love them! Ned was a short fat man with a bloated face and a massive head of mousey brown hair. He had tiny little pin-sized eyes beneath hugely puffy eyebrows which gave him the appearance of Barney Rubble after fifteen rounds with Muhammad Ali. His wife Carol – as Agnes had remarked once to Carmel Dowdall – had a face that looked like a cow licking piss off a nettle, and the children, God bless them, looked like a collection a three-year-old child would draw in a picture. Still, they were good-hearted people, who had previously lived in Sheriff Street, and the bonus for both Agnes and Carmel was that Ned was a baker. He worked in St Joseph's bakery just off North Frederick Street. His starting time was 4.30am, and he had a car. So the two 'girls' would join Ned every morning on his city-bound trip, both women sitting in the back of the Volkswagen Beetle where they could still see the road ahead clearly, as little Ned's head came just above the dashboard. Mark continued to cycle into work, downhill all the way to the city and uphill on the return journey, although this never seemed to bother him. Rory, now recovered from the beating, rode safely and soundly in and out of the city centre on the Number 40 bus.

Dermot struck up a friendship with the eldest Brady

son, Patrick, whose nickname was 'Buster'. Physically, the two had little in common, Dermot now becoming more handsome by the day and with an athletic physique, and Buster probably two stone overweight and looking like he was going to explode at any moment. However, Buster was a very happy young fella and laughed at every one of Dermot's jokes. Over the next year they would grow to be best friends, Dermot enjoying the role of becoming Buster's protector and Buster idolising the very ground Dermot walked upon. The six other Brady children were all girls, and this left Buster in the same position as his father – oppressed. It also meant that he had to join the girls' activities and, although he hated it, every Monday and Wednesday Buster was marched off to Irish dancing classes and every Saturday or Sunday he would be entered into a Feis somewhere in the city. Dermot attended a number of these competitions, where Buster never won anything, but Dermot got great fun out of seeing this little blob bounce around the stage in a kilt and cape with the other children trying to stay out of his way. Dermot once told Buster he looked like 'a fuckin' roundabout', and, true to form, rather than feeling insulted, Buster laughed heartily and agreed with him.

Buster, for his part, attended every football match Dermot played in, where Dermot always seemed to score and where Buster could hear the older men on the line exclaim every so often that Dermot was 'beautiful on the ball'. Buster now spent more time in the Browne house than he did in his own, and Agnes suspected that it was more than just Dermot's company he yearned for ... often she would catch him entranced as he looked at Cathy.

Cathy Browne and Cathy Dowdall, heading towards

their sixteenth birthdays, were blossoming into beautiful young girls. Boys from the adjoining roads of Casement, Barry and Mellowes, began hanging around Wolfe Tone Grove. Some boys even ventured up to Wolfe Tone Grove from as far as Ballygall Parade and McKelvey – both in East Finglas. This could be a treacherous trip, because in Finglas, as in the city centre, the tribal system soon took over and East did not see eye-to-eye with West. Still, these boys believed it was worth it in the hope of getting off with two of the beauties of Finglas West.

For their part, the girls enjoyed the attention and, although Cathy Browne was a little bit shy, Cathy Dowdall made up for that with her ebullience and openness. In fact, one could describe her as a flirt! The girls would kiss selected boys, Cathy Dowdall more enthusiastically than Cathy Browne. The main difference between the two girls was that Cathy Dowdall was looking for a good time whereas Cathy Browne was looking for someone to love. This probably explained the shock on Cathy Browne's face one evening as she sat on the corner of her bed digesting what Cathy Dowdall had just announced.

'A feel? You're goin' to give him a *feel*?'

'Yeh! A feel.'

'Why?'

''Cause – 'cause I want to.'

'Well, what if yeh get pregnant?'

'Don't be stupid, yeh can't get pregnant from a feel – can yeh?' A little uncertainty crept in at the end.

'I don't know.' Cathy Browne's grasp of the facts of life was a bit wobbly.

A short silence followed. Cathy Dowdall did not meet with Cathy Browne's eyes.

'Anyway, I already let him feel me diddies,' she proceeded defiantly.

Cathy Browne said nothing, just threw her head back and roared with laughter.

'What are yeh laughin' at? I did!' Cathy Dowdall insisted.

Cathy Browne stopped laughing and looked at her friend. 'Cathy, yeh don't have any diddies.'

'Well, me nipples, then, I let him feel me nipples. It was lovely, Cathy.'

Cathy Browne reddened a little, not really wanting to know the details of the other Cathy's nipple escapade. Instead, she moved the conversation along.

'So when? When is this *feel* goin' to happen.'

'Tonight, I suppose.'

'Well, I hope you know what you're doin'.' Cathy Browne ended her side of the conversation with a tremor in her voice.

* * *

David Molloy was fifteen and a half years old, he would be sixteen in five months' time. He was born in a third-storey flat in a building at Number 1, Synott Place which lay to the south of the Mater hospital. When he was just six years old the building in which he lived was condemned and his family became one of the early settlers in the new town of Finglas, which was only just beginning its sprawl. His street, Mellowes Road, was the last outpost of civilisation then, for behind his home for miles and miles ran wheat-fields, golden every summer as far as the eye could see. On their arrival in Finglas his mother enrolled him in St Fergal's Boys' School which he attended up until his thirteenth year. He then left and went on to secondary school in the newly built Patrician College on Dunsink Road in Finglas.

David had always felt a little closer to God than to his friends. The move to the Patrician College brought about his introduction to the Patrician Brothers, men who had vowed celibacy and dedicated their lives to God and to the education of youth. This had a profound effect on David and after only his first year in the college he announced secretly to Brother Francis, his religious knowledge instructor, that he felt he might have a vocation. Brother Francis had been very calm and understanding with the young boy – vocations from the pupils of Patrician colleges throughout Ireland were not a rare thing, but neither were false vocations or perceived vocations. Brother Francis told David that he was very young to make such a bold decision, that he should dwell upon the thought and pray to God for guidance. He should also in the meantime live the life of a normal young boy as much as possible, and as Brother Francis put it, 'Put your vocation to the test.' This David Molloy had faithfully done for the last year. Little was he to know that this night, the night of his second date with a pretty girl from Wolfe Tone Grove named Cathy Dowdall, his vocation was about to undergo its greatest test yet.

The two of them sat in the balcony seats of the Casino cinema in Finglas village. There was a double bill, the first movie, *Imitation of Life*, had brought sniffles from every corner of the theatre. Now, midway through the second film, *Madame X*, the audience cried openly as Lana Turner opened the bedroom door to bid her child a silent farewell. David sat sniffling. Cathy, her arm linked into his left arm and her head resting on his shoulder, was not sniffling – instead, she was beginning to panic. Halfway through the second film and he hasn't even fuckin' kissed me yet, she thought to herself. She looked up into his face; a thin rivulet was running down his cheek and his eyes were locked on the silver screen. Cathy realised that if she was going to make any progress this night with her 'feel' she would have to get the ball rolling herself.

'I'll be back in a minute, I have to go to the jacks,' she whispered into David's ear.

He smiled at her with tear-filled eyes and nodded his head. Half-crouching, she made her way past the eight people between her seat and the end of the row, and headed for the ladies'. There were two other girls there, one standing at the sink smoking, the other busy at the mirror applying the 'war paint'. Cathy went into one of the cubicles and locked the door.

Quickly she removed her knickers, white cotton airtex, and rolling them into a tight ball held them in her fist. She flushed the chain in the toilet and exited from the cubicle in time to leave the ladies' with the other two girls. When she was back seated beside David she snuggled into him once again.

The movie still commanded his full attention. Lana Turner was now roaming the snowy streets mistaking every young boy for her own lost child. It was all very moving. Cathy nudged David and grudgingly he took his eyes from the screen and looked at her.

'Look what I have!' Cathy said in a hushed voice as she held out her hand containing the knickers. She opened her fist and the knickers seemed to bloom like a posy on a sunny morning. David looked at them, puzzled for a moment.

'I took me knickers off for yeh,' Cathy smiled.

David smiled too. He took the knickers from her hand and began to mop his tears. As Cathy stared at him incredulously, he then blew his nose.

'How thoughtful of you, Cathy,' he said half-sobbing.

Cathy thumped him in the gut and snatched the knickers back. 'Yeh filthy bastard, filling me knickers with your snots, what'll I tell me Ma? I took them off so you could do it!' she explained, still in a hushed voice – although it brought a couple of 'shushes' from the surrounding audience.

'Do what?' David whispered.

'Feel it!'

'Feel what?'

'So you could feel me cherry!'

For a moment David said nothing. 'But ... I don't want to feel your cherry,' he said finally.

'I do!' a voice from behind him announced.

'Fuck off, you,' Cathy snapped back to the voice in the dark.

She sat in silence for a moment. David returned his attention to Lana Turner. Cathy's thoughts drifted away. She had read somewhere that some men are slow to respond to sexual advances by women and in these cases a little bit of coaxing would be required. Fearing the film would end soon, and her chance would be gone, Cathy got straight down to the coaxing. She leaned across David's lap with both hands and slowly undid the zip on the fly of his charcoal grey Patrician College trousers. When she looked up into David's face she had on a leering smile. David, on the other hand, had his eyes wide open in shock. She began to rummage around the snow-white jockey Y-fronts until she found the little opening and carefully slipped her hand in. She again looked up at David's face. He now had his eyes tightly closed and his lips were barely moving. At last her hand found its target. Pulling the flap of his Y-fronts to one side, she extracted his now erect pecker.

'Ooh! Hail Mary full of grace the Lord is with Thee ...' David began to pray aloud.

Suddenly there were shushes all around. A girl's voice yelled, 'Shut the fuck up.' By now David had a tremor in his voice and his knuckles were going white on the arm rests.

Cathy was stunned for a moment, then she noticed the usherette arriving down the steps with the flashing torch, the beam going in all directions. Quickly Cathy sat back into her seat as the torch began to move along the row. It first passed, then quickly returned to settle on David's fly. Cathy took a sideways glance at the point of attention of the light. David Molloy looked a sight, his eyes tightly closed, perspiration running from his brow, and gripping the arms of the seat like he was about to take off. His little penis was protruding from the grey trousers and when the light settled upon it, it looked like a little cabaret singer – one expected it to break into 'My, My, My Delila' any moment.

Cathy Browne was in tears the next day as Cathy Dowdall told how David Molloy was taken from the cinema by the scruff of the neck up the aisle with his pecker hanging out. Undeterred over the next few years, Cathy Dowdall went on to better and bigger things. David Molloy remained traumatised for some time, yet the night did one good thing for him, it confirmed his vocation.

As the years went on, Cathy Browne would fondly recall the adventures that Cathy Dowdall brought into her life and would live each one by proxy. We should all have a Cathy Dowdall in our lives.

The Browne family spent the following couple of years settling into their new home and finding their feet once again. Despite her earlier reservations, Agnes began to enjoy Finglas. The air was clearer here and every day there was a growing sense of community spirit. For the time being, all was well with the Brownes.

PART 2

Chapter 11

LONDON 1975

MANNY WISE COULDN'T BELIEVE HIS LUCK. He had found him. He had found him quite by accident in a kebab shop right across the road from the entrance to King's Cross station a year ago. Manny was down at the station browsing through the latest batch of young ne'er-do-wells for some fresh recruits, and having had no luck decided to treat himself to a donor kebab. Manny sat in one of the cubicles, with his kebab and a paper cup of coffee, his back to the door and looking down the counter at the line of people waiting to be served.

He knew the minute he saw the young man that he was different. Although a bit dirty, obviously from some months on the street, he was handsome and had a good physique. This boy, Manny thought, looks after himself. He watched the young man take his place in the line and noted how his eyes drifted from customer to customer. The young man eventually chose his prey. It wasn't what he did that impressed Manny, but the way he did it. What ends the career of most thieves is that they are consumed by their own greed. This lad was not greedy. The target was a young lady in a leather miniskirt and wool jacket. She was accompanied by a handsome, tall, middle-aged man. They had had a few drinks and seemed happy in each other's company. The young homeless man's removal of the girl's purse from her handbag was pure poetry in motion – fast, smooth and professional. But it was what happened next that most impressed Manny. He watched the young man closely. He very quickly opened the purse, removed some notes, but not all of them, from the wallet section, closed the purse and stuffed the notes into his pocket, then he waited. The happy couple paid for their take-away meal and as they moved towards the door the young man called after them in a Dublin accent, 'Excuse me, missus?'

The girl turned on her heel. 'Yes.'

'You dropped this.' The young man proffered the purse.

The girl slapped the side of her handbag and opened it as if not believing it was her purse. She then gave him a broad smile. 'Why, thank you very much, that's very kind of you.'

'Nice one, mate, appreciate that!' the girl's escort added and winked.

The young man smiled shyly and said, 'Don't mention it,' and returned to his place in the line.

Manny was very impressed. He rose from his seat and went to the counter, skipping the queue, and asked the young lady for another coffee. As the girl was making the coffee up for him he drifted down the line, leaned over to the young man and spoke very softly. 'I saw that, mate, – work of art, different class ...'

Manny then returned to the top of the line, collected his coffee and sat back down in his cubicle. As the line moved up the young man stared at Manny. When he came abreast of where Manny was seated, Manny invited him over. 'Get your stuff and sit down here, mate. You and me should have a talk.'

'Are you fuzz?' the young man asked.

This elicited a howl from Manny. 'If I were fuzz, mate, I'd have 'ad the bracelets on you and you'd be in the back of a fuckin' squad car ten minutes ago! Get your stuff and sit down 'ere.'

They sat talking and drinking coffee for two hours. The young man gave his name as Ben Daly, although Manny suspected that this was not his real name. Manny didn't care, he liked him, a lot!

'You're not greedy, son, I like that!' Manny said.

'I do okay,' the young man answered.

'Well, how would you like to do a whole lot better than okay?'

'What would I have to do?'

'A little bit of this, a little bit of that.'

'For you?'

'Yeh! For me, my son. What you do now is Mickey Mouse stuff. I'll put you in the big league. You'll be my right-hand man.'

'So that's what you want me to do for you – what can you do for me?'

'Get you out of those shitty clothes for a start, sonny boy. Take yeh down to Saville Row, get yeh a bit of decent gear. My right-hand man has to look a bit of spiv. And, of course, put a few bob in your pocket. Life can be flash when you've got a bit of cash! Know what I mean?'

Ben Daly's cold blue eyes never left those of Manny Wise.

Manny figured he'd done enough. He'd made his pitch;

he'd made the man a decent offer. He began to stir his coffee and waited for his answer.

After a few moments Ben Daly's face cracked into a smile. 'Mr Wise, looks like you've got yourself a right-hand man.' Ben extended his hand and the two shook hands warmly.

Over the next few weeks, Ben Daly, or whatever his name was, began working for Manny. He was quick to learn, intelligent, and at times very, very funny. Manny would often muse that in essence Ben was a typical Dubliner. Unlike the other kids that Manny had recruited in the past, Ben did not jump straight onto the drugs trail, in fact it took some months before Manny convinced the young man to try a snort of cocaine. But once he got into it, Ben loved it, and Manny and Ben would have a couple of drinks and a snort and a good laugh most weekends. As the famous tobacco manufacturer John Player once said, 'If you're hooked, you're hooked!'

Over the following months Manny managed the young man very carefully. He would pose little tests for the lad, giving Ben opportunities here and there to skim a little cash for himself or to stash some coke for himself. But Ben never did, seeming to be content to walk in Manny's shadow and nibble on the crumbs of the 'good life'. Manny was ecstatic. He had at last found his right-hand man. Little by little, Manny began to trust the young man further and further, until eventually he trusted Ben to go and meet the Amsterdam connection himself.

Ben lived in a small bedsit over a TV rental shop in Harlesden, a predominantly black area. But he never seemed to have any trouble, and built up a nice little cocaine and heroin outlet for himself. Manny Wise began to relax and depended on Ben more and more as time went on. For his part, Ben Daly never let Manny Wise down. They were, it seemed, of like mind and like kind.

Chapter 12

DUBLIN 1974

'HAPPY BIRTHDAY, DEAR MA–ARK, happy birthday to you.'

There followed a communal cheer. Mark was embarrassed and looked every inch of it. He stole a sideways glance at Agnes. Tears welled in her eyes but she looked very proud.

'Blow out the candles, Mark!' Betty shrieked.

Mark was holding Betty's hand as he leaned forward towards the cake, which was shaped like a big twenty-one, and with one large puff extinguished all the candles. This again was met with a huge cheer, and to Agnes's delight the DJ blasted out Cliff Richard singing 'Congratulations'.

Agnes was pleased she had decided to have Mark's twenty-first birthday party at home. The back garden was certainly big enough for the marquee, which Mark had paid eighty pounds to rent. What had formerly been the coal shed was now the bar. It was manned by Dermot and Buster Brady. They had managed to procure a cooler and some kegs of Guinness from – God knows where!

The cooler was actually on loan from the Carrick Inn, the local pub, and the kegs were courtesy of Guinness and the CIE freight train service.

This was a sort of black-market income for Dermot and Buster. They would go down to the canal at Ratoath Road where the train line ran parallel to the canal. On leaving Dublin, the train would build up speed, and as it got to Glasnevin, because it was now going through a housing area at night, the driver would kill the engine and coast along that stretch of track. The driver would not accelerate again until he reached Blanchardstown. Buster and Dermot had devised a plan. As the train slowly coasted along past Glasnevin cemetery they would jump aboard. The train was made up of forty to fifty carriages, all stacked with Guinness kegs. The trick then was to lean on the middle kegs and with both feet push one of the outside kegs off the train onto the bank. The boys would push one each, then jump off the train before it had time to accelerate, and walk back along the track, collecting the two kegs and rolling them home across the fields.

They had built up a great relationship with the owner of the Carrick Inn and, although he would have taken an unlimited supply, the two boys confined themselves to a keg each a week. Things didn't always work out according to plan, of course, and on more than one occasion Buster found himself forty miles down the line in Portlaoise, freezing cold and trying to hitch home in the early hours of the morning. Still, the risk was worth it and it provided much-appreciated pocket money for the two boys who, although working – Dermot in a local factory making barbed wire, and Buster in the same bakery as his father as a trainee baker – still found good use for the money.

Rory had brought a new friend, Dino Doyle, along to the party. Like Rory, he was a qualified hair stylist and, like Rory, he was homosexual. Agnes was unaware of Rory's homosexuality and still held out hopes that he would meet a nice girl some day and settle down. Indeed, Rory had tried to tell her on one occasion. It was on one of Rory's midweek days off. Agnes had taken the day off as well, and Agnes and he sat in the kitchen having a quiet cup of tea.

Rory looked up into his mother's face. 'Mammy?'

'Yes, luv, what is it?'

'I want you to know something ...'

Agnes smiled at her son. 'Yes, luv, what do yeh want me to know?'

Rory hesitated before breaking what he knew would be earth-shattering news to Agnes. 'I ... I'm gay, Mammy.'

Agnes held onto her smile and said casually, 'That's nice – I'm happy too,' and she stood up and began to clean the kitchen.

Apart from Frankie, who Agnes knew wouldn't be there, both Cathy and Simon were also missing from the party, albeit temporarily. Simon was on late shift at the hospital where he was now a senior porter and would arrive back to the house at about 10pm, still in time for the 'shenanigans'. Cathy had slipped out of the party momentarily to go two doors up to Cathy Dowdall's house, where Cathy was putting her young baby to sleep. Nobody in Wolfe Tone Grove, nor indeed in Finglas, was surprised when Cathy Dowdall became pregnant just a year ago. Cathy Browne had lost count of the amount of false alarms her best friend had had before eventually falling prey to the 'joys of motherhood'. Her baby, Emmet, now three months old, was a beautiful child, and both the Cathys doted on him.

Cathy Dowdall's mother had stuck by her daughter throughout the pregnancy and the birth, and although young Cathy never revealed who the father was, she made the concession of lying to her mother by telling her that the father was a solicitor. This made her mother feel a lot better, thinking that, illegitimate or not, the child would at least have some brains. Cathy Dowdall didn't dare tell her mother the real truth, that Emmet's father was, in fact, a butcher from the meat counter in the local supermarket. Carmel Dowdall was never to find out her daughter's secret and never even asked where the 2lbs of bacon, 1lb of homemade sausages, 2lbs of mince, a Sunday joint and a chicken came from every Saturday.

Baby Emmet was a bit restless and Cathy Dowdall said she would hang on a little longer before returning to the party. Cathy Browne hurried back as she was expecting her own special guest. While Cathy Dowdall's search for a good time resulted in the birth of a beautiful baby, Cathy Browne's search for love had come to fruition too, she believed, about two months ago when she met Mick O'Leary. It was love at first sight for both of them. They had seen each other virtually every day since their first meeting, sometimes during the day, sometimes at night, depending on how Mick's shift was working. Mick came from Bishopstown in Cork, and was in Dublin only because his job had taken him there. This coming weekend Cathy was to make the trip to Cork to meet Mick's parents, but tonight it was Mick's turn to be introduced to the Browne clan.

As Cathy was rushing back to Number 43 and the party,

she saw the shadowy figure of a man walking towards her half-way up the street. His swagger made Cathy think it might be Mick and this was confirmed when he called her name. His step got a little quicker and when they eventually met at the gate of the Browne household they hugged each other and kissed passionately.

'Sounds like a hell of a party,' Mick said, nodding towards the house.

'Yes, it is. You're about to meet the Brownes at their best – or worst?' Cathy said demurely.

'Well, you've talked so much about them, Cathy, I feel I know them all already. So come on, let's go and meet the Browne brood.'

Cathy giggled, and holding hands the two of them entered Number 43. They looked into the front room which was jampacked with the older neighbours. Peggy McDonald was very drunk and treating the audience to a rendition of 'Frankie and Johnny'. Peggy was just coming to an important line in the song for which she leaned down to her husband's face and spat out: 'That there ain't no good in men!' This brought a huge cheer from the women in the room and howls of laughter from the men. Cathy and Mick withdrew quickly.

In the hallway Mick looked up the stairs and saw a young boy sitting on the top step. He had what appeared to be a sketch pad on his knees and his hands were working furiously.

'Who's that?' Mick asked.

'That's me youngest brother, Trevor. He just keeps drawing all the time – I think he's a bit slow,' Cathy answered, and pulled Mick towards the back door where the main action was taking place. They went down the two steps to the back yard and Cathy walked over to the bar where Buster and Dermot were now pissed drunk and trying to sing 'Chirpy Chirpy Cheep Cheep' in harmony with the record that was playing in the marquee.

'Dermo! Dermo! Where's Mammy?' Cathy called over the din.

Dermot turned to Buster and said, 'Buster, is my face red?'

'Red? No, Dermo, your face isn't red.'

'Then she mustn't be up me arse.'

The two exploded into laughter, wrapping their arms around each other as only drunk men can.

'Dermo, I'm serious, where's Mammy?' Cathy was now a little annoyed.

Dermo copped on. 'Sorry, Cathy, I was only messin'. She's inside somewhere – you go in and get her and I'll give your man a drink!' he offered.

Cathy squeezed Mick's hand. 'D'yeh mind, Mick?'

'Not at all! You go and get your mother, girl, I'll have a chat with the barman.'

Cathy vanished into the marquee and Mick stepped up to the bar.

'What'll it be, sham?' Dermot asked.

'Oh, a pint of Guinness, I suppose, seeing as how yeh have it there.'

'We have Guinness, we have Smithwicks, we have Harp, we have any draught yeh want, sham, isn't that right, Buster?'

'That's right, Dermo.'

'Browne and Brady, purveyors of fine draught beers,' Dermot chuckled as he began to pull the pint.

With two-thirds of the glass full, he placed the pint on

a drip tray to allow it to settle. Dermot now turned his full attention to Mick.

'So, sham, you're the boyfriend we've all been hearing about?'

Mick smiled. 'Well, be Jaysus, I hope so. Otherwise I've wasted a lot of money over the last couple of weeks entertaining somebody else's girl.'

Dermot laughed heartily, liking the man immediately. 'I can tell by your accent that you're not from Dublin. Where are yeh from?'

'Cork,' Mick said simply, and nodded towards the pint which was now ready for topping up.

Dermot took the pint up, pushed the pump handle forward, and began to top off the creamy pint of Guinness. He placed it in front of the foreigner from Cork and continued with the questions.

'So, tell us, what's your name, sham?'

Mick picked the pint up, studied it as a first pint should be studied, then answered, 'Well, me name is Michael, but the boys in the station call me Mick.' And he began to take a long mouthful from the cool pint.

'Well, then, Mick it is! Now listen, Mick, if ever yeh need a bit of cheap gear – station? What fuckin' station?'

Mick withdrew the glass from his mouth and carefully and slowly licked the white creamy moustache left on his top lip. He then smacked his lips and turned his face to Dermot. 'Finglas Garda Station, I'm a Garda there.'

Dermot could have done with some help from Buster as he stumbled backwards, but Buster was doing his best to stand up straight while still throwing up behind the two stolen Guinness kegs. Mick O'Leary smiled and took his pint to the doorway of the marquee.

He arrived just in time to meet Cathy, who had her mother by the hand, and Agnes in turn held Pierre by the hand. The trio stepped outside the marquee into the fresh night air to meet Cathy's boyfriend. Cathy made the introductions.

'Mammy, this is Mick.'

Agnes looked up into the face of the man, and at that moment for the first time realised that her daughter was now a woman. His features were plain, with the exception of a slightly oversized, pointed nose. His smile was toothy and his handshake was warm. Agnes smiled at him.

'You're welcome to our home, son, I hope you're lookin' after my daughter.'

'Be Jaysus, missus, I'm minding her like the crown jewels,' Mick replied, and held onto his smile.

Pierre coughed. Cathy took over once again. 'Mick, this is Pierre. He's my mother's ... my mother and Pierre are ... he's kind of like a father to us,' she finally settled on.

Pierre beamed. Had she had a month to prepare, Cathy could not have picked an introduction that would have flattered him more. Pierre extended his hand, and Mick took it and shook it warmly.

'It's very nice to meet you, Pierre.'

'It is also very nice to meet you. I have tremendous respect for men in uniform. I wore a uniform myself, you know ... yes indeed, when I served with the French Foreign Legion.'

Agnes interrupted. 'Don't mind him, Mick, he's full of shite.'

'No, no, my darling, it is true,' Pierre exclaimed.

'Sure it is, Pierre luv. Next ye'll be tellin' me that ye're really James Bond and you're only workin' in the Pizza

Parlour as a fuckin' cover.'

Mick and Cathy burst out laughing. Pierre pretended to be hurt, but also saw the joke.

'Here, Pierre, take Mick over to the bar and get him another drink. I want to have a word with me daughter,' Agnes instructed.

Pierre put his arm around the young man's waist, for his shoulders were too high, and guided him back towards the bar, while beginning a story of how he had single-handedly captured six Algerian terrorists with only a toothbrush and a Gillette razor as weapons. The mother and daughter looked at them as they walked away.

'Well, Mammy, what d'yeh think?'

'He looks all right. But Jesus Christ – a guard! I don't know, Cathy.'

'Ah for Christ's sake, Mammy, it's a job, not a disease.'

Agnes turned towards her daughter and looked into her face. It was a face she recognised well – she had seen it in a mirror twenty-four years before. She took both of Cathy's hands in hers.

'Tell me, sweetheart, what do *you* think?' Agnes asked.

For a moment Cathy dropped her eyes, then, lifting her head, she returned her mother's glance.

'I know it's only a couple of months, Mammy, but I think I love him.'

Agnes squeezed Cathy's hands a little tighter. 'And when he kisses yeh, luv, d'yeh feel a little feather runnin' up and down your spine?'

'Yeh! I do!' Cathy answered excitedly, not realising that anyone else would have felt this.

'Then you've found the one – and don't you ever let him out of your sight, luv.' Agnes said this with a big smile and went to let go of Cathy's hands, but Cathy held on a little longer.

'Is that what you felt, Mammy? With Daddy – the feather runnin' up and down your spine?'

Agnes's smile was a sad smile. 'No, luv. With your father it was an ice cube. I didn't get the feather 'till I met Pierre. Now come on, let's go and get our men.'

Cathy gave her mother a huge hug and the two 'girls' went to join their partners.

There followed a couple of hours of singing and dancing and the night air above Wolfe Tone Grove was filled with laughter and merriment as the drunken crowd celebrated the twenty-first birthday of a good man. Agnes Browne was filled with joy and pride in her family, and although the ferry had taken a small piece of her heart across the water to England, what was left of that heart now overflowed with happiness.

Rory danced crazily with his friend Dino – the two lads obviously didn't have any luck with the girls that were there, Agnes thought. Cathy sat on the lap of her Garda boyfriend, and they talked and looked at each other as if the rest of the world had ceased to exist. Mark celebrated the official age of becoming a man, though Agnes knew that this boy had been a man since he was fourteen. Dermot and Buster Brady for some reason were upstairs, putting things into the attic, and Trevor was sound asleep in his bed.

Suddenly the music stopped and Agnes heard the DJ blow into a microphone and announce: 'Ladies and Gentlemen! A bit of quiet, please. We'll have a few words from the man of the moment – Mr Mark Browne.'

The announcement was greeted with a huge cheer

intermingled with a bit of friendly name-calling from Mark's football team-mates, and as Mark took the microphone, Agnes rose from the back step and walked to the doorway of the marquee to hear his speech.

'Ladies and Gentlemen,' Mark began, only to be met with jeers and calls of 'Go on outa that!' Mark laughed but went on. 'Friends and family! I can't thank yis all enough for the many presents I've received. It's great to see so many friends here, both from town and from Finglas, in our new home. I asked the DJ to let me speak for two reasons, and neither of them were to make a speech. The first reason was to say thank you, not the one I just said, but a special thank you to a very special person.' All heads turned to the doorway where Agnes Browne stood. Betty went behind the DJ stand and returned with a huge bouquet of roses. Mark took the bouquet from Betty, cradled it in his right arm and continued his speech. 'I have here in me arm a bouquet of roses – there's twenty-one yellow roses and three red ones. I want to explain what they're for. The twenty-one yellow roses, Mammy, are to remind yeh of where yeh were and what yeh were doin' twenty-one years ago. I hope I was worth it.'

Agnes stood in the doorway and just slowly mouthed, 'Yes!'

'The first red rose, Ma, is to say thanks for all yeh gave up to try and make things better for us.' There was now total silence in the marquee. 'The second red rose, Ma, is from all of your sons and your daughter to remind yeh how much we love yeh – and the third red rose, Ma, is because I wanted an extra one in the bunch 'cause I want you to know that if I could round up all the roses in the world and gather them into this tent here tonight, you'd still deserve one more.'

Agnes walked to her son and gave him a hug. She took the flowers and held them close to her like a new-born child. She embraced Betty and their tears mingled, and suddenly she was surrounded by neighbours and friends – and trying to feign indifference.

Mark once again got the attention of the crowd and when he had reasonable silence continued his speech. 'I'm not finished yet. I would also like to announce that with the permission of Mrs Collins and me Ma – tonight me and Betty are gettin' engaged.'

This was met with a huge cheer, and while the crowd clapped and roared, Mark smiled and slid a single-stone engagement ring onto Betty Collins's wedding finger. She was immediately surrounded by every teenage girl in the tent and whisked away to a corner where the ring would be perused, tried on, and spun in wishes. Right on cue the DJ hit the button to play, yes, once again, Cliff Richard singing 'Congratulations'.

Chapter 13

LONDON

IT HAD BEEN A VERY CLOSE SHAVE. Manny sat in the holding cell of Maidstone police station. It had been too close. He had gone to Maidstone to meet a new client, taking with him a small sample of heroin and a small sample of cocaine. Maidstone was well out of his area and he didn't know a lot about the place, so maybe he should have known better. Manny, however, was not adverse to a bit of expansion and when the opportunity came to have a sub-distributor in Maidstone, he thought: What the heck?

The meeting had been set up for a lane at the back of premises called The Silver Skillet. The Silver Skillet was an up-market eatery with cabaret. As Manny sat on the side of a dustbin, awaiting his rendezvous, he could hear the stand-up comedian rattle them off upstairs. The place was in an uproar of laughter. Whoever the comedian was, he had them by the balls.

Manny saw the police car slowly pass by the end of the lane. It didn't stop, but instinctively Manny got up and began to walk further down the alley. He didn't see the policeman at the other end, but thankfully the constable had forgotten to turn off his radio and once Manny heard it crackle he took off like a jack-rabbit. He sprinted through a pedestrian shopping area. All the shops were closed and shuttered and his footsteps echoed loudly around the concourse. So too did those of the now-pursuing constable. Within two minutes Manny had reached his Sunbeam Rapier. He slammed the door, turned the ignition and gunned the engine, flung the car into first gear and screeched out of the shopping-centre carpark.

After three minutes of hard driving the view in Manny's mirror was clear. He exhaled, relaxed and eased his foot off the pedal. Suddenly out of a side road the black police Jaguar pulled in behind him with the blue light flashing. Manny took a sharp left and gunned the engine again. The police car broke hard and didn't make the bend. The driver had to reverse to get it to right itself. It then followed at speed. The short overshoot by the police car had given Manny enough time to open his passenger window and toss out the two little bags. He watched in his mirror as the police drove past the spot where he had dumped them. He then took a sharp right, followed by the police car. Just a couple of hundred yards into this street, Manny indicated and pulled over. Four policemen jumped from the car. It had been a set-up.

Manny's window was now rolled down and as the first officer reached him, Manny very said coolly, 'Is there a problem, officer?'

Manny was taken from the car, handcuffed and brought to Maidstone Police Station. They searched him thoroughly – very thoroughly – and found nothing. They then put him in a cell while half a dozen officers went back and retraced the route Manny had driven, searching the area as thoroughly as they could to see if he had ditched the drugs. They found nothing. Somebody had got an ounce of cocaine and an ounce of heroin, but it wasn't the Maidstone police force. On their return to the station the officers removed Manny from his cell and formally charged him with dangerous driving. Before they had locked Manny up they had taken his personal belongings. One of the officers counted the money in Manny's wallet, and it held two hundred pounds, so they now posted his bail at two hundred and fifty pounds. Manny was given his one phone call – they led him to a room, placed a phone in front of him and left him alone. Manny dialled the number carefully and hoped that Ben would be there.

Ben Daly was half-asleep, sitting in front of the television he had rented from the shop below his bedsit when the phone rang. He walked to the hall outside the flat where the public phone hung and answered it.

'Hello?'

The caller was Manny Wise.

'Manny, what's up?'

'Ben, mate, I'm in a bit of bovver, I'm in the nick.'

'Jaysus! Why, what happened?'

'It don't matter now. I'll fill you in on all that later. For now I need you to get some dough. Do you have fifty quid?'

'Fifty quid! Jaysus, no. I have about seven quid, that's all, Manny!'

'Have you still got the spare key to my apartment?'

'Yeh.'

'Right, then, here's what I want you to do ...' Manny gave Ben strict instructions on how to open the safe's combination lock. Begin at zero, go eighty-two to the right, back to zero, spin all the way around to the right, back to zero again, then go eighty to the left, and then go back to nine on the right, and then turn the locking handle. He told him to get fifty pounds in cash from the safe and to take a further twenty quid to cover a taxi fare out to Maidstone Police Station. Ben could tell from the way Manny's final instruction, 'Move your arse!', was delivered that our Manny didn't have the bottle for a prison cell.

When Ben walked up the Edgeware Road he saw the police car parked outside the Chinese restaurant. He checked his pocket for the small torch he had brought and ducked down an alley to go into the apartment through the back door. He climbed the two flights of stairs up to Manny's place, slid the key in the lock and quietly turned it. The door opened easily. He didn't need a torch to find his way to the study.

Before tackling the safe he checked from the corner of the window that the car was still in place. It was. He crossed the room and bent low to the safe. Ben had never opened a safe before in his life, but he followed the instructions Manny had given him to the letter. He was surprised when the safe opened first time. As the door opened wide, so too did Ben's eyes. There was stacks of money! Manny had told Ben to bring along the fifty quid and some identification for Manny. He had told him also to make sure to bring his Irish passport which was in the back of the safe. Ben reached over the money and lifted a tray at the back of the safe. The first thing that caught his eye were two neat foil-wrapped parcels, one marked 'CC' the other marked 'HN'. Ben knew exactly what these parcels contained. Underneath the parcels were some stocks, bonds, some official-looking papers and a yellowed envelope on which was written 'Dublin Papers'.

Ben opened the envelope, read the page and then returned it to the envelope. He sat for a few moments just staring at the money, his mind clicking. Finally he made his decision. He took Manny's passport and into it he slid fifty pounds in sterling. He then took the two foil-wrapped parcels and stuffed one into each pocket of his anorak. He took a fistful of money, which later turned out to be three thousand pounds and rammed it down the belt of his trousers. He closed the safe and left.

When Ben Daly arrived at the night desk in Maidstone Police Station it was 2am. He handed the desk sergeant Manny Wise's passport along with the fifty pounds Manny was short for his bail. The sergeant did not like Ben Daly.

'Who are you?' the sergeant asked.

'I'm the man who just gave you the passport and fifty pounds,' Ben answered very coolly.

'And what's your name?'

'Why?'

'Let's just say I'm interested.'

'Well, you should get interested in butterflies, they're easier to catch.'

The desk sergeant gave up. Within minutes Manny Wise was collecting his personal belongings, including an empty wallet, and he left the building with Ben. They didn't speak till they were safely cocooned in the Sunbeam Rapier and heading down the motorway towards the city.

'You're a good mate, Ben, I knew I could depend on you,' Manny said without taking his eyes off the road.

'No problem, Manny,' Ben answered, and he too stared straight ahead.

'Those fuckers – I think I'll be giving Maidstone a miss,' Manny laughed.

'Yeh,' Ben answered, and he too laughed.

When the laughter died down Manny leaned across and tapped Ben on the back. 'Let's go back to my place, Ben, we'll snort a line and have a couple of laughs. What do yeh say, mate?'

'Nah, Manny, not tonight, man. I'm really tired. If yeh just drop me off in Harlesden I'd appreciate it.'

'Sure, Ben, sure.'

'Yeh don't mind, Manny, d'yeh?'

'No, no way, Ben, I really am very thankful for what yeh did tonight, Ben. You're a good mate, and I'll show my appreciation in the right way at the weekend.'

'Ah it's nothin'! Sure, you'd do the same for me, Manny,' Ben swiftly put in, half-knowing this was not the case.

After dropping Ben off, Manny drove straight back to his apartment on the Edgeware Road. The police car was still there and as he locked his car Manny gave the policemen a little wave. They looked back at him, their faces full of scorn. Manny laughed loudly and slammed the front door of the building.

On the first floor an apartment door opened, and the head of an elderly man popped out. 'I say, there, is it necessary to make so much noise each time you enter the building?' he asked. It was obvious from his tone that he had once been a man of authority, probably army. Never the less, it had taken him months to pluck up the courage to confront this man who lived in the apartment above his own. Like the other residents in the building the old soldier knew exactly who this man was and how dangerous he was. But, enough was enough, a man had to make a stand sometime.

Manny climbed the first flight of stairs to where the old

man was and put his face right up to the old guy's. 'If you don't like it, Pop, then fuckin' move.'

The man closed his door without reply. He was shaking.

Manny bounded up the remaining stairs and noisily let himself into his apartment. He removed his coat, tossed it on the couch, went to the stereo and pushed a button. Lights came on and the speakers came alive with Nat King Cole singing 'When I Fall In Love'. Manny then went to the drinks cabinet, filled a crystal glass with ice and poured a good four fingers of Scotch into it. Even as he took his first swig he was walking towards the bathroom. He gave the knob one swift turn, the shower gurgled and then began to spit out hot steaming water.

After his shower, Manny came from the bathroom with a towel wrapped around his waist, a second smaller towel which he used to dry his hair in one hand and the Scotch in the other hand. He placed his glass on the table, bent down, and whirled the combination wheel of his safe. As soon as he opened the door he knew there was something wrong. He could tell instinctively that there was a good wadge of money missing, and when he reached his hand back into the darkness to where the tray was, he could feel no foil-wrapped packages. He stood erect and screamed, 'The bastard!'

Nearly four hours had passed since Manny had dropped Ben Daly off at the TV rental shop. Manny stood in front of the apartment door above the shop. He leaned his back against the wall, raised his leg and slammed his heel into the door just above the lock. It flew open. Manny found exactly what he expected to find. Ben Daly, or whoever he was, was gone.

For the next few days Manny had his runners scouring London for Ben Daly. He also hired a couple of thugs to keep round-the-clock watch on both Heathrow and Gatwick airports. He even got in touch with some mates of his in Liverpool who had agreed, for a small fee, to shoot down to Holyhead for a few days and keep an eye on the departures there. Manny was convinced that Ben Daly, like all animals on the run, would head for home.

Luckily, Manny had a photograph of Ben. It was a shot taken by one of those sidewalk photographers as he and Ben were leaving The Mean Fiddler one night. He had copies of the photograph made and distributed to all the runners. He tried over the next few days to keep business going as normal, but Ben's betrayal was eating through his stomach like acid. Every spare moment Manny Wise had, he spent either at the train stations or at one of the airports in the hope that he would see Ben.

Three weeks after Ben's disappearance hopes of finding him were looking grim. Manny had called off the Liverpool boys, his city runners had all come back with no good news and Manny had taken to just dropping by the airports himself the odd time.

'Some day – you little bastard!' Manny mumbled to himself as he walked across the concourse at Departures in Heathrow terminal. He was looking for a newsagent's to get a paper. He went into WH Smith's, only to find they didn't have a *Standard* left. The girl suggested that their shop down in Arrivals might have one, so with nothing else to do, Manny took the escalator down.

He was halfway down when he saw him. He had dyed his hair and had cleaned himself up, but there was no doubt about it, it was Ben Daly. Manny kept cool. At the bottom of the escalator he half-hid behind a circular pillar and watched as the disguised figure of Ben Daly walked up and down, glancing at his watch. When the figure turned his back to Manny, Manny quickly began to move towards him. The flick-knife in his hand up his right sleeve clicked and the gleaming stiletto-like blade barely protruded from his hand.

Fuck you, Ben Daly, Manny thought as his anger built up. The distance between the two of them closed. Manny nearly wished that Ben would turn around, he wanted to see his face as he pushed the blade into his heart. When Manny was within fifteen feet of his target the young man suddenly spun around and called, 'There you are!' to a much older, also well-dressed man.

The young man and the older man hugged each other and Manny could now see the young man's face very clearly. It was not Ben Daly. He had very nearly stabbed the wrong man.

'Fuck! I'm gettin' paranoid,' he mumbled to himself, and beads of perspiration popped out on his brow.

The young man caught his gaze and looked at Manny, puzzled. Manny quickly spun on his heel and headed for the newsagent's.

I wonder what *he* wanted? Mark Browne thought, gazing after the peculiar-looking man who had stared at him as he embraced Greg Smyth at the Arrivals gate. But the thought soon left his mind as Greg broke into an apology.

'I'm terribly sorry, Mark, the traffic was horrendous.'

'It must have been, Greg, it's not like you to be late.'

'Well, the car's outside – let's go,' Greg began to usher

Mark from the Arrivals building. But instead of moving towards the door, Mark began to look around the building.

'Tell me, Greg, do yeh know if there's a postbox here?'

'Why yes, Mark, I think it's over there by the foreign exchange.'

'Just give me a minute, will yeh? I have a letter to post.'

Mark had used the time while waiting for Greg Smyth in deep thought about his mother. Although she never discussed him, and his name was never even mistakenly dropped in conversation, Mark knew how much Agnes longed to believe that some day Frankie would return, successful, and with a good explanation as to why he had partaken in the beating of his younger brother and stolen his mother's money. No amount of explaining would ever erase the disgust Mark felt every time he thought of Frankie. Yet he knew that if the scenario were to occur, as remote a possibility as it was, that he would earnestly welcome Frankie back, but only because he knew how happy it would make his mother. For a few moments the thought fleetingly – very fleetingly – crossed his mind as to whether it would be possible for him to track Frankie down in London and convince him to contact home. Suddenly Mark had an idea. He went to the WH Smith newsagent's in the Arrivals building and bought a card. Using his left hand, he scribbled a little note on the inside, inserted forty pounds in English money, then addressed the card to Mrs Agnes Browne, 43 Wolfe Tone Grove, Finglas West, Dublin 11. This was the letter he needed to post before departing for business with Greg Smith.

The three-day business trip went well for Mark, but still he was happy to get back. Greg Smyth had upped his order, and Mark had finally convinced the Army and Navy Stores to begin taking supplies of the newly designed Elizabeth suite. The store presumed that the suite was named after their good queen, and Mark allowed them to think this, knowing it was better than their knowing that it was actually named for a young Betty Collins back in Dublin. Mark had his briefcase on his lap and was reviewing the order dockets as the taxi sped him towards Dublin's city centre. He made a point on returning from his business trips always to go straight to the store of Wise & Co. Bespoke Furniture, and inform Mr Wise and Sean McHugh of how he had done. The two men now stood well back from the business end and allowed Mark, who was now Managing Director of the company, to plough ahead.

Still, when Mark arrived back from his trips, Sean and Mr Wise would go over the order dockets as if (a) they understood and (b) they felt that what they thought would actually make a difference to this dynamic young man. It was a little game all three played and was enjoyed equally by all parties.

This time Mark arrived at the store in Capel Street only to find that Mr Wise had been taken ill that morning and was now tucked up in a bed in the Bon Secours hospital, a private hospital on the north side of Dublin.

'He took one of his turns,' Sean explained, sounding a little more worried then usual.

With a player missing, they didn't bother with the usual game and at 5.30pm Mark helped Sean lock up the shop and he got the bus home to his mother's.

When Mark sat down to his tea he was joined by his mother, Trevor, Rory, Dermot and Cathy. Agnes, who was always bright and cheery in the company of her children, seemed to have an extra bounce in her step tonight. Mark barely noticed this as his mind was on Mr Wise. The opening of the shop in Capel Street was just a temporary respite, and although Mr Wise had certainly perked up a lot in the initial months of his working in the shop, this had been as short and sweet as an ass's gallop. He then went through a period of highs and lows. One day he looked as if he would run a hundred-yard sprint, the next you wondered if he could walk across a room. Eventually, the lows outnumbered the highs, and Mr Wise shortened his working week to one or two days. His 'turns' were more frequent than ever and it seemed as if he constantly had a small pill beneath his tongue. Mark tried to shake the thought of a sick Mr Wise from his head and focus his attention on young Trevor.

'How's school goin', Trev?' he asked.

Trevor had his elbow beside his plate and his head resting on his hand, and he didn't look up. 'Okay.'

Trevor was the only one of the Browne family that was not a talker. Conversations with him were usually one-way traffic and his answers were as short as possible, if not entirely monosyllabic.

But now Trevor did look up. 'I have a letter for yeh, Mammy.'

'A letter for me? From who?' Agnes frowned.

'From Miss Conway,' Trevor said flatly.

Miss Conway was the principal of St Mary's school where Trevor went. In her mid-fifties, it was unlikely now that she would ever marry. Monday to Friday she devoted herself to the school, tirelessly working on the young children in an effort to open their minds to the possibilities and opportunities that could lie before them. Miss Conway believed that there was no such thing as a bad child. She was a strict disciplinarian, but even the worst of the children regarded her as fair, and the rest positively adored her. She was a branch secretary of the newly formed Greenpeace, an organisation working for a better environment throughout the world. She also spent part of her weekends teaching Traveller children, visiting halting sites all over Dublin city and the surrounding areas. She was a prominent member of Victor Bewley's Travellers' Trust.

Agnes regarded her as a weirdo and always referred to her as the 'Do-gooder'. Trevor left the table and returned with a manila envelope, which he handed to his mother. Agnes tore open the envelope and read the short letter.

'Christ – now what's wrong?'

'What is it, Mammy?' Mark asked.

'She'd like me to drop up tomorrow, to have a little chat about Trevor.'

Agnes put the letter down on the table and scolded Trevor. 'What have yeh done now?'

'I dunno.' Trevor looked back down at his plate.

Everybody went back to eating their dinner. After a couple of moments Agnes reached into her apron pocket and took out an envelope. 'Speakin' of letters – I got this this morning.' She held up the white envelope.

Mark recognised it immediately. 'What's that, Mammy?' he asked.

'A card. From Francis,' she announced proudly.

All heads lifted from their plates simultaneously and in unison the family said, 'Frankie!'

'That's right – Francis.'

'Where is he? What's he doin'?' Cathy asked.

'Doin' very well for himself. Workin' as a travellin' salesman, he says. Will I read it to yis?'

Mark poured himself another cup of tea, and tried to sound as indifferent as possible. 'Sure, Ma,' he said, 'if you want to.'

Agnes took the card from the envelope. On the front it said 'Thinking of you, Mother' above a bouquet of flowers. Agnes read this aloud as if it were poetry. And then she began. '"Dear Mammy, I'm so sorry I have not written in such a long time. What happened to Rory was a mistake, but even so I should never have been a part of it, and I will never find enough words to tell Rory how sorry I am."' Agnes looked at Rory and smiled. 'He's sorry luv,' she told him, in case he hadn't heard what she'd read. Then she went on. '"Can you ever forgive me for takin' your bingo money? The only explanation I can offer is that I was frightened and knew I had to leave the country. I had no money, so I took what was there. If it takes me forever I will pay you back. I enclose forty pounds as a first payment."'

Agnes now delved into her apron pocket and held aloft two English twenty-pound notes, moving them in a circular motion around the table so that each one of the children would have a chance to see them. Again she smiled and put the forty pounds back in her pocket.

'"I am workin' as a travelling salesman, so there is no point in me givin' you a return address, I move so often. But I will be in touch again, soon. Love, your son, Francis."'

Agnes closed the card and Mark once again saw that twinkle in her eye that had been missing for so long.

'Here, let's see it, Ma,' Dermot asked and took the card

from his mother's hand. He studied it for a few moments and over the top of it he peered at Mark. Mark caught his gaze and dropped his eyes. Dermot knew about things. He closed the card and handed it back to his mother.

'Well, that's great, Mammy. At least we know he's well, it'll stop you worrying so much.' Dermot went back to his tea.

'Yes,' Agnes said to no-one in particular, and she held the card to her breast.

That night Mark Browne and Cathy Browne both headed out on dates, Dermot called in for Buster Brady and the two of them headed off for a game of snooker to the Cross Guns Snooker Club in Phibsboro. Rory took Trevor to a movie. So it was that Agnes was alone when Pierre called for one of his early visits, knowing he had to be back at the Pizza Parlour before eleven o'clock. Agnes had told Pierre that day about Frankie's letter. Pierre knew how important this letter was to Agnes and he was pleased with the mixture of excitement and relief in Agnes's tone. He arrived at the house with a bottle of champagne and he was prepared for a celebration. He was not prepared, however, for what he got! Agnes was on such a high that the champagne vanished within a half-hour of Pierre's arrival. They sat side-by-side on the Loretta suite, and Agnes snuggled up to Pierre.

Suddenly, and without any announcement, Agnes began to unbutton Pierre's shirt. She ran her fingers through his soft downy chest hair, and Pierre's nipples popped up like two little tin-hatted soldiers peeking out of fox holes. They kissed passionately. Pierre had his arms wrapped around Agnes. Just above his thumb he felt the zipper of her dress. Slowly he pulled the zip midway down Agnes's back. He gently slid his hand in a circular motion over her baby-soft skin and she shuddered to his touch. She wore no bra.

Pierre now decided to go for gold, and finding the zip again he pulled it down to its finishing position at Agnes's buttocks. Agnes had been hugging Pierre with both her arms wrapped around his neck and she now removed her arms. Pierre had expected this, he couldn't even believe he had got this far. He expected Agnes to put her hands behind her back and without breaking the kiss re-do the zip midway up her back, if not all the way. Instead, while still kissing him, Agnes took a half step back, dropped her arms to her sides, and the dress slid to the ground.

So it was that night that Agnes Browne, a widow with one child engaged, one nearly engaged, and at forty-one years of age, had, in a Corporation house in Finglas, her very first 'organism', and the man she was with had two.

Chapter 14

AGNES HATED THESE VISITS to the principal's office. She'd had one or two courtesy of Dermot and, God knows, Frankie'd had her up to the school so often that some of the teachers thought she was staff. Miss Conway's office was neat and tidy as Agnes had expected, but instead of the smell of dusty books and stale cigarette smoke that Agnes usually associated with a principal's office, Miss Conway's had a beautiful aroma of Estée Lauder. Miss Conway entered the office very busily. She looked every inch the school principal.

'I'm terrible sorry to keep you waiting, Mrs Browne.'

'That's all right, luv, what's up?'

'I want to talk to you about Trevor.'

'I guessed that. He's the only one I still have at school,' Agnes smiled.

Miss Conway didn't see the joke. 'Quite so. Mrs Browne, your son is showing an amazing propensity for artistic endeavour.' She dropped it like a bombshell. But it might as well have been a water balloon, for Agnes hadn't a clue what she was talking about.

'What d'yeh mean? Eh ... Miss?' Agnes asked.

Miss Conway placed her elbows on the desk, put her

hands together as if she were praying, and put her fingers against her lips. She was considering the best way of illustrating her point to an obviously puzzled Agnes Browne.

'Take a look at that window, Mrs Browne,' Miss Conway began, pointing to the window behind Agnes.

Agnes turned in her chair and looked. What had once been a plain school window about eight feet wide by four feet high had now been painted in stained-glass style with the scene of the Last Supper. The colours used were stark and exciting, and the meal which was to be the basis of the Christian rite looked like a celebration rather than the wake it was usually depicted as. The artist obviously had a different spiritual point of view to the one most commonly held. The window was beautiful; on a sunny day one could imagine this office filled with colours. The work of art also served to distract one's attention from the fact that there was a large crack, half-moon shaped, in the top right-hand corner of the window. Agnes turned back to Miss Conway.

'What about it?' She asked.

'Your son did that!' Miss Conway announced proudly.

'The little bastard! I'll fuckin' kill him! How much will it cost to replace?'

Agnes hadn't seen the painting, all she had seen was the crack. This is a common thing with parents of gifted children.

'The painting, Mrs Browne. Your son did the painting.'

Agnes spun around again, and this time she saw the painting. Slowly she stood and walked to the window. She gently laid her hand upon the figure of Matthew, who was pouring wine for Judas. She turned her head to Miss Conway. 'My son did this?'

Miss Conway beamed a smile. 'Yes, Mrs Browne, Trevor did that. Mrs Browne, I honestly believe that in Trevor we could have another Monet, Picasso, Salvador Dali ...!' Miss Conway was glowing.

Agnes stared at her blankly for a moment, hoping the names Miss Conway was rattling off were artists and not terrorists. Agnes again returned her gaze to the window and slowly walked backwards to her seat and sat down hard.

'That's why I asked to see you, Mrs Browne. You see, I have a friend in the National College of Art. I've already shown him some of Trevor's work and he too believes the child is gifted, so I would like your permission to send Trevor there immediately. I think he should start working with oils and acrylic as soon as possible. What do you think?'

'How much will it cost?' Agnes asked carefully.

'I believe I can secure a grant from the Arts Council. Talent like Trevor's is a national treasure,' Miss Conway assured Agnes.

Having granted her permission and signed the necessary application forms, Agnes left the school a happy mother. Walking back home, she racked her brain trying to figure out where Trevor's talent had come from. She decided that the only candidate was Uncle Gonzo, the plumber, he was great with his hands.

Agnes waited until everyone had finished their tea that evening before making the announcement that Trevor would be attending the National College of Art, and that Miss Conway regarded him as a national treasure. Everyone clapped and congratulated Trevor, who just shrugged it off.

After bingo that night in the Carrick Inn, Agnes retold the entire encounter with Miss Conway to Carmel Dowdall. Now, it might have been the high of the last couple of days that caused Agnes to overstep her usual two glasses of cider. The drinks just seemed to be going down very fast and the lounge boy was replacing them as quickly as the girls were downing them. By the time they left for home they'd had five or maybe six each, and were a little tipsy. They rounded the corner of the Carrick Inn to go past the chip shop. There was a single lamp outside this chip shop and a group of men, about twenty or twenty-five of them, stood around it in a circle, playing pitch-and-toss. As Agnes got closer to the group she saw two young lads standing in the middle and recognised Dermot's voice, as he cried, 'Heads a half a dollar.'

Agnes screamed, 'Dermot Browne, are you playin' in that toss school?'

Agnes had got it slightly wrong. Dermot and Buster were not *playing* in the toss school, they were running the toss school. Quickly and without reply, the two young men gathered their money off the ground and scampered across the field towards home. The group of men were displeased. Dermot and Buster were obviously up a few bob.

'What did yeh do that for?' one of the men grumbled.

'You should know better, yeh big bowsey. They're only chisellers,' Agnes replied, her speech slurred.

'Yis go on home to yiser wives,' Carmel Dowdall added to the attack.

'Go on out of that, yis pair of fuckin' drunken wagons,' another voice called from the group, and the men laughed.

Agnes stood unsteadily, with her hands on her hips, and Carmel Dowdall linked on to her – the blind leading the blind.

'I'll have youse know ... my daughter is goin' out with a guard ... and one of me sons is a Managing Director ... don't you call us wagons!' Agnes declared.

The two women turned to walk away and over her shoulder Carmel Dowdall added, 'Yeh! And one of her chisellers is a national fuckin' treasure, so there.'

With that, Agnes and Carmel haughtily trotted off into the darkness.

Chapter 15

LONDON

THINGS HAD NOT GONE WELL for Ben Daly in the six months since he'd stroked Manny Wise. The three thousand pounds he had stolen disappeared quickly. He gambled some, drank some more, and even lost seven hundred and fifty pounds of it from his pocket while he slept on top of a cardboard box in a lane one night, in a drunken, drugged stupor. He sold the cocaine for a pittance, and all of the heroin he used himself. What little remained would last him no more than three or four days. He had no clothes except what he wore on his back. The pants reeked of stale piss and the jacket of drug-induced vomit.

His hair was now long and matted, and he had a beard and moustache, which made his sunken cheeks and eyes even more pronounced. The veins in both his legs and both his arms had collapsed, with so many puncture marks tracked along them – one would think someone had run a sewing-machine across them. He was now reduced to injecting the heroin under his tongue.

His latest fix was beginning to take hold. He felt better – in a while he would feel wonderful. He sat on the steel steps that ran down to the basement of a dry-cleaning shop. It was after 2am but still the dry cleaner's was working flat out and the warm air coming up from the extractor fans was comforting. He tucked his hands beneath his arms, turned up his collar and leaned against the red-brick wall. He closed his eyes and as so often before his thoughts drifted to home.

He thought of the quays of the river Liffey, filling his nostrils with the smell of roasted hops coming from the Guinness brewery. He floated over Henry Street and saw the colourful shoppers smiling and laughing, and the music from Golden Discs on the corner of Mary Street drifted up to meet him. He passed Moore Street – but didn't go down Moore Street, no not Moore Street, he wouldn't go down there, he couldn't. Not now. Not ever again.

As the potent drug began to take its full grip on him, he felt warm and wonderful, and a huge smile crossed his face. But salt tears flowed like fountains from his eyes. A few more days and then what? Ben Daly would cross that bridge when he came to it.

Chapter 16

'IT'S LIKE HEUSTON STATION IN HERE,' Agnes roared as Dermot crawled beneath her legs looking for a missing shoe.

'Stay easy, Ma, will yeh?' Rory told her for the fiftieth time.

Rory was blow-drying Agnes's hair. He'd already done haircuts on Mark, Dermot, Trevor and Buster Brady, and a trim, layer, and bob on Cathy. Everybody's hair was ready for the wedding except his own. Rory looked over his shoulder at Dino, who was now putting on Trevor's bow-tie.

'Dino, will you do mine when I'm finished here, will yeh?' Rory asked his friend.

''Course I will, love,' Dino replied.

The 'love' had slipped out. Rory shot Dino a glance and Dino grimaced, but the entire thing went completely over Agnes's head. Rory then looked at Mark – it hadn't gone over Mark's head. Rory blushed. Mark walked over to him, a serious look on his face, and put his hand on his brother's shoulder.

'As long as you're happy, Rory,' he said simply, 'that's all I care about.'

'I am, Mark.'

'Good.'

Mark went back out to the kitchen to make yet another cup of tea, for yet another visiting neighbour. For a man who was to be married in an hour and a half, Mark was remarkably calm. His brothers were running around like headless chickens trying to put all the pieces of their tuxedoes on as if they were jigsaw puzzles. The neighbours had been coming and going since early morning. This was traditional in a Dublin home on a wedding day. Mark made two cups of tea and carried both of them upstairs to the boys' bedroom where Simon was standing in front of a mirror with a sheet of paper in his hand.

'A ... A ... A ... And the Lo, Lo ... Lord J ... J ... Jesus sa ... sa ... said unto them ...'

'Here, Simon, here's tea.' Mark placed the mug on the dressing-table.

'Ta ... ta ... thanks, Mark.' Simon sat on the bed and took a sip of tea.

'Yeh don't have to do this, Simon,' Mark tried to ease the pressure on Simon.

'I wa ... wa ... want to, Ma ... Mark,' Simon declared.

'Then, I want you to.' Mark smiled at his brother.

The turmoil was no less frantic in the Collins household. Mrs Collins wasn't in the tea mode. She had cases and cases of bottles of Guinness. She had expected ten or fifteen callers that morning, but her sitting-room now resembled a rush-hour bus in Calcutta. There was barely room to move. It seemed that every customer she'd ever had had decided to pay a visit. Still, with Mark and Betty paying for their own wedding, the least she could do was lay on a decent spread at home, and she had certainly done that.

Cathy was upstairs in the bedroom with Betty, helping her to dress, as the chief bridesmaid should.

'Did yeh take a look at Pierre's face?' Cathy asked Betty, looking at her in the mirror.

It had been a close shave for Pierre. When the eventual plans for the wedding were announced, the first thing Pierre noted was that he would not be taking the place of the father figure of the Browne family at the top table. This duty Mark had entrusted to Rory, with Dermot as best man, and Simon as groomsman. Mark immediately saw the disappointment on Pierre's face, so he quickly carried on, 'Oh, Pierre, Betty and I have a special favour to ask of you.' Mark took Betty's hand.

Pierre tried to show interest and hide his disappointment at the same time, expecting a request from the happy couple that he should stand outside the church as people arrived and give them flowers or some such menial task. Instead it was Betty that spoke.

'Pierre, I know how attached you are to the Browne family, but I wonder would it be possible just for one day to be my father – and give me away?' She smiled. So did Pierre. His spirits lifted immediately. There could only be one thing better than being a father figure to the groom and that's the father of the bride. He would get to walk down the aisle with a beautiful young woman on his arm, decked out in white. Pierre was overcome and accepted readily. That night he and Agnes celebrated with yet another bottle of champagne, and a couple of 'organisms' thrown in for good measure. Pierre now stood downstairs among the throbbing crowd in the Collins sitting-room, with a smile on his face that looked as if it had been put there by plastic surgery.

At three o'clock precisely, Mark and his three brothers sat in the front pew before the altar in Gardiner Street church. Although it was cool outside, the sun beamed through the stained-glass windows, and every conceivable colour was spread out along the church walls. Suddenly somebody said, 'She's here.'

Three of the boys swivelled their heads immediately, but not Mark. He suddenly stiffened and for a moment the enormity of what he was about to do washed over him. The organist struck up 'Here Comes The Bride' and everybody stood up. That moment of panic that every groom knows lasted just a couple of seconds.

Slowly Mark turned his head to look down the aisle. Betty saw him turn, and smiled. She wanted to cry but she held back the tears. Not so Pierre, who sniffled all the way up the aisle. Mark took in the vision that was his bride. Her satin dress had a layer of delicate hand-woven lace over it. The pattern of the lace was of tiny roses and each rosebud had a pearl stitched to the centre of it. It had taken Betty nearly two weeks to sew on over a hundred of these tiny pearls. For a moment she walked into the blazing sunshine as it beamed through the stained glass and Mark's heart leapt. Surely, he thought, God has sent me an angel.

The ceremony went without a hitch. Then came the reading. Simon got up and climbed the steps to the podium. He had been practising in front of a mirror for weeks now, convinced that a large intake of breath followed by a slow delivery would minimise, if not completely eradicate, his stutter. As he took his place and opened his little booklet, everybody sitting on the Browne side of the church took a large intake of breath.

'A letter from St Pa ... Pa .... Paul to the Corinthians.' For a moment everybody's heart stopped, but Simon went on and completed his reading without one more falter. When he had finished and closed the booklet, Agnes began to clap. She was quickly joined by the rest of the Browne family and then by the entire congregation, the Collins side clapping even though they didn't know why. At the reception in the Maples hotel in Drumcondra later, over thirty people approached Simon to congratulate him on such a well-read lesson.

The meal of melon wedge, vegetable soup, and stuffed turkey and ham, followed by sherry trifle and tea, was quickly devoured by the one hundred and twenty guests attending the wedding meal. Finally, a teaspoon was hammered against a glass and the room fell into silence for the best man, Dermot Browne.

Dermot stood up and began his speech. 'Ladies and Gentlemen, Rev. Father. Yis are all very welcome here today to celebrate Mark gettin' his leg over.'

Nobody laughed except Buster Brady. Agnes's thunderous look to Dermot was enough to tell him there were to be no more remarks like that.

'What does he mean?' the celebrating priest Fr Simmons asked Mrs Collins.

'Ah, it's somethin' to do with the tradition of steppin' over the broom, Father.'

'Oh I see, very interesting.'

Dermot's speech became shorter than he had intended it to be as he stuck now to the bare essentials, thanking the priest for a lovely ceremony, thanking the bridesmaids for looking so beautiful, thanking the hotel for a 'lovely bit of grub' and thanking the guests collectively for the lovely wedding presents that Mark and Betty had received. He then moved on to the telegrams and cards. Needless to say, there was one from Dolly in Canada, from Greg Smyth in England, and from Mr Wise, who couldn't be there because of ill health and was still confined to the Bon Secours hospital. Mark's heart sank a little bit at this one as his thoughts drifted back to the kindly man laughing heartily as he spoke to a snotty-nosed little boy outside of the turf depot all those years ago. The next, and last, telegram brought a smile to Agnes's face. Dermot read it aloud.

'"Congratulations and best wishes to both of you on your wedding day and wishing you future happiness always." And that comes from Francis Browne in London – that's me brother,' Dermot announced and glanced sidelong at Mark's puzzled face. This last telegram was greeted with a round of applause and under cover of the noise Dermot said from the corner of his mouth to Mark, 'Two can play at your game', and he winked.

Mark smiled and looked down the table at his glowing mother. The meal was followed by a tremendous celebration. Most people got drunk. Old friendships were renewed and as is traditional on large family occasions in Dublin, many hatchets were buried for the day. At ten o'clock that evening, as the party was in full swing, the new Mr and Mrs Mark Browne departed in Mark's new company car for their honeymoon in Galway. They had planned a two-week honeymoon, the first week in Galway, the second in Killarney. However, circumstances were to interrupt Mark's honeymoon when it was just eight days old.

* * *

Nurse Maureen Clifford's foam rubber heels squelched as she walked along the quiet midnight corridor of St Thomas's ward. It was so quiet that even the noise of her nylons could be heard as they rubbed together at the knees. She stopped quite suddenly. The sound of the cardiac alarm was piercing. It was coming from behind her. She spun around. The light over the door of room seven was flashing on and off. In two strides she made it to the wall phone, dialed zero, the emergency number, and called 'Cardiac arrest, room seven.' Then she quickly replaced the receiver.

By the time the cardiac team arrived, no more than fifty seconds later, she'd already opened the pyjama jacket and was pumping the chest with her palms. Her efforts failed and as the cardiac team burst into the room she stepped well back. The gel packs were quickly opened, applied to the chest and to the terminals of the electrodes. They were placed on the chest, the doctor shouted 'Clear', and the tiny body suddenly leapt in the bed. All eyes turned to the monitor. It still showed a straight line. They tried the procedure again and again for fifteen minutes. At exactly twenty-two minutes past midnight Dr William Deegan declared Benjamin Wise officially dead.

Chapter 17

THE FUNERAL WAS WELL ATTENDED at Mount Sinai, a Jewish cemetery on Dublin's southside. Sadly, there was only one man who cried at the funeral. Mark Browne was consoled by his bride of only ten days. Benjamin Wise's only son Manny was there also, but there were no tears from him. When the burial rite was over, Mark walked up to Manny Wise and extended his hand. Manny's hand was like a dead fish.

'I'm sorry for your loss,' Mark said – though really things should have been the other way around.

'Yeh! Eh sure – Mark isn't?'

'Yes, Mark Browne. I'm the Managing Director of your father's – well, I suppose your company now.'

They began to stroll towards the cars.

'The furniture business? Yeh – that's right,' Manny said. 'What d'yeh reckon it's worth, Mark?'

The question surprised Mark. 'In what sense?'

'In the sense of what would I get if I sold it?'

'It's not that kind of factory, Mr Wise. Your father's factory has very few assets. Its real worth is in what it can produce. And it can produce reasonable quality furniture at the right price for a long time to come. You won't be dissatisfied with the books. Why don't you come down and have a look? I'll go through them with you,' Mark offered.

'Nah! I'm not in the furniture business, Mark. I'll probably just close the place and sell off the property. Unless, of course, you want to buy it?'

'I wouldn't have that kind of money, Mr Wise.' Mark was now worried about the futures of the forty-two men who were employed by Senga Furniture.

The two were joined by a much older man. Mark thought he recognised the face, but couldn't place him. Manny Wise had no idea who the man was at all. The man took Manny's hand, offered his condolences and introduced himself. 'My name is David Jacobson, Mr Wise. I was your father's solicitor.'

Mark remembered him. He extended his hand. 'Hello, Mr Jacobson.'

'Hello, Mark, good to see you again, son.'

The elderly man turned his attention once again to Manny Wise. 'It's my understanding that you are resident overseas, Mr Wise, so perhaps expediency will be appropriate in the matter of your father's will,' he suggested.

'A will?' Manny was perplexed.

'Oh yes. Mr Wise senior left a will and, as was his way, everything is correct and proper. May I suggest a reading early tomorrow, say ten-thirty in the morning? Would that suit both of you?' He looked from one man to the other.

'Both of us?' Mark enquired.

'Yes, Mr Browne. Mr Wise left explicit instructions that you were to be there for the reading.'

'And what about me?' Manny asked. 'Did he leave any instructions about me?'

'Oh, I think he knew for sure that you would be there.' Mr Jacobson delivered this jab without so much as blinking.

The funeral was not like the traditional Irish funerals that the Brownes were familiar with. They stood around, waiting to see which pub the crowd would be adjourning to, only to see them scatter away in their cars.

'That's no way to pay your respects!' Dermot stated.

'They have different ways,' Sean McHugh explained, the breath coming from his mouth like fog.

'Well, fuck the different ways, let's send him off our way,' Dermot insisted.

There were nods of agreement all round and the Browne family along with the entire staff of Senga Furnishings made their way into the city centre to Foley's pub and betook themselves to alcohol. As the afternoon progressed, there were many tales told of moments of kindness by Mr Wise. Sean McHugh had an audience for a full thirty minutes as he told of the heartbreak young Manny had caused his father over the years. This was met with a lot of 'tut, tuts,' and comments like, 'Little brat' from the older members of staff and 'Smarmy bollix' from the younger ones. As more drink was taken the atmosphere lightened and the ballads began. During the fourth verse of Sean McHugh's rendition of 'James Connolly', Mark slipped out of Foley's. He tucked his scarf down, turned his collar up and stuffing his hands into his pockets he began to walk around the area of his birth. He soon found himself standing outside the turf depot. Across from it was the tiny terraced cottage in which the kindly old man had spent his years. For a moment Mark saw Mr Wise framed in the doorway of the cottage. He could see the old man wearing six cardigans and in his outstretched palm the two-shilling piece reward he had given to the young Mark every Saturday for lighting his fire.

'Jesus Christ, Mr Wise, where's the cocoa now that I need it?' Mark said aloud and began to cry.

He sat on the small turf depot wall for over an hour, but now reliving the happy thoughts and memories he had of the man who in so many ways had replaced his father. He then made his way back to Foley's where he proceeded to get absolutely blind drunk. He arrived home to his 'new' flat on the North Circular Road in the early hours of the morning. He went to bed fully dressed and as his young wife cradled his head like a little baby, Mark sobbed himself to sleep.

He awoke to the crackle of rashers frying in the kitchen. The aroma was beautiful and he felt good until he moved. The pain in the back of his head and right down his spine was excruciating. He groaned.

'You're up then?' Betty asked from the doorway of the bedroom.

'What hit me?' Mark asked weakly.

'Life!' Betty said simply.

'Is it late?'

'Yeh, I suppose it is, for you. It's ten minutes to ten – but that's all right because last night in Foley's pub you gave all the staff the rest of the week off, on full pay!'

'Did I?'

'Yep!' Betty smiled at him.

Mark lay back down again gingerly, and put his hands over his eyes. 'Well, they deserve it. They're going to have a lot more than the rest of the week off if Manny Wise has his way.' Suddenly he sat bolt upright.

'Manny Wise!' he said aloud. 'Jesus Christ, what time did yeh say it was?'

'Ten to ten,' Betty answered.

Mark jumped from the bed, forgetting the pain. 'The will! Christ! Jacobson's reading the will this morning at half-ten. Where's Jacobson's office?'

'Will? Office? Slow down, Mark, what are yeh talkin' about?' Betty was confused.

Mark closed his eyes for a moment and gathered his thoughts. 'Mr Wise left a will, apparently, with his old solicitor, David Jacobson. It's being read this morning at half-ten and Mr Wise left instructions that I was to be there for the reading. Christ, where's me brown suit?'

Betty went to the wardrobe, took out a brown suit, bent down, picked out a pair of brown suede shoes, then walked to a tallboy and extracted a clean white shirt and a tie.

'You're going nowhere, Mark Browne, until you've had a cup of tea. Now, you get dressed and I'll put the kettle on. In the meantime I'll go through the 'phone book to get an address for this David Jacobson fella.'

By now Mark was hopping around the room on one leg trying to get the other one into the leg of his trousers.

Manny Wise was already sitting in the waiting room of David Jacobson's office when Mark arrived.

'Good mornin', Mr Wise,' Mark said.

'Yeh! Good mornin', son,' Manny Wise answered.

The super-efficient Thelma, Mr Jacobson's secretary, looked Mark up and down. 'Mr Browne, I presume?'

'Eh ... yes. That's right. Mark Browne.'

The woman picked up the telephone receiver, pressed a button and announced, 'They are both here now, Mr Jacobson.'

She stood up. 'Follow me, please.'

David Jacobson obviously had a big firm. The corridor was long with about six offices off it. The name on every office door except one ended in Jacobson. The odd one out was a Maxwell. Maxwell must have married Jacobson's daughter, Mark thought to himself, as he strolled behind Manny Wise down the long corridor. The two men were led into a large meeting room into which David Jacobson entered simultaneously from another door.

'Good morning, gentlemen. Please sit down,' Jacobson invited.

When the three were seated, David Jacobson unbound a file and extracted a yellow sealed envelope. He laid it face down on the table, then passed it to the two men and asked them to witness that the seal had not been broken. Mark nodded and slid it to Manny Wise.

'Yeh, yeh, yeh! Get on with it, mate, I've got a plane to catch,' Manny agreed, and he pushed the envelope back to Mr Jacobson.

The solicitor opened the envelope, extracted a single sheet of paper and read the following. 'I Benjamin Wise being of sound mind residing in Number 2 Cornell Cottages in Dublin's city centre make this as my final Will and Testament.

'I presume that there are three or at least two sitting in audience as my solicitor David Jacobson reads this Will. Sean McHugh may not be there but this is no matter for I know my words will be communicated to him faithfully by David Jacobson. Mark Browne I know is sitting there for I left explicit instructions that he should be and he has never failed to carry out my instructions. For this I thank you, Mark, and I thank you also for the care, kindness and warmth you have always shown to me. I want you to know too that it has been your courage, honesty and tenacity that has kept me alive as long as I have stayed alive. I hope you miss me now, for I would surely be missing you were these roles reversed, but I ask you to think of the happy times we had together and know this – that they were the greatest moments of my life. I thank you, Mark.

'Manny, you little shit! I want you to listen closely to my will.' Mr Jacobson did not raise his eyes from the paper as he read that piece.

'So here we go. To my first employee and longest friend on this earth, Sean McHugh, I leave my home, unencumbered by mortgage or debt. It is not fit to be lived in, but I hope he will sell it and that the proceeds of this sale will make his closing years as comfortable as his friendship made mine.

'My only other assets are the premises and business of Senga Soft Furnishings, formerly Wise & Co., and the retail shop premises in Capel Street known as Wise & Co. Bespoke Furniture. My interest in these, the Property and Deeds of both premises, and indeed the business, though I am embarrassed to say this for the business was never mine but belonged to the man who made it, all of this I leave to Mark Browne. My only request of him being that he has as much thought for the staff within these businesses as I have taught him to have.

'To my son, Manny, I leave all he ever wanted – his own ego. I hope the two of you are very happy together.

'Signed Benjamin Wise.'

Mr Jacobson folded the paper slowly and looked up. 'So, there you have it, gentlemen,' he announced.

Mark did not know what to say or do, so he just sat still

at the giant conference table, staring at his folded hands in front of him. Suddenly, Manny Wise burst into laughter. Mark jumped with fright and Mr Jacobson frowned.

'You find this funny, Mr Wise?' Jacobson asked. It obviously was not proper to laugh in a solicitor's office at the reading of a will.

Manny Wise took a cigarette from a pack, lit it, exhaled, and drummed his fingers on the table. 'Yes, I do find it funny, Mr Jacobson. Tell me, when was this will made?'

'Two years ago in 1973,' Mr Jacobson answered quite solemnly.

Again Manny Wise burst into laughter. 'Then it's not worth shit, Mr Jacobson.'

Mr Jacobson became indignant. 'How dare you, Mr Wise. I assure you this will is perfectly legal and was drawn up with the greatest of integrity by myself and witnessed by my secretary, Thelma, isn't that so?' He turned to Thelma who nodded her assent, at the same time giving Mr Wise the evil eye.

Manny stood up. 'My father cannot leave something to someone that he does not own,' Manny said these words very carefully.

Jacobson was now confused. 'Can you be more specific, Mr Wise? What are you saying?'

'I'm saying that in London I have a document dated prior to this will in which my father signed everything over to me, for love and natural affection.'

'I don't believe it!'

'Believe it, Mr Jacobson, believe it!'

'I refuse to believe it. Mr Wise made me well aware of his relationship with you. He would hold no truck with your involvement in his business affairs.'

'I have the document, Mr Jacobson.' Manny now virtually sneered.

David Jacobson sat quietly for a couple of moments gathering himself. The outburst was uncommon for him and he now returned to his calm, cool solicitor mode.

'All right, Mr Wise, I will give you until Friday at three o'clock to produce the said document here in this office. If we can verify your father's signature on such a document then I will suggest a number of law firms you should go to to contest this will. However if by three o'clock on Friday this supposed document is not produced, then I shall execute the will post haste.'

Manny Wise began to laugh again and made his way to the door.

Jacobson called after him. 'Are you clear on that, Mr Wise?'

Manny placed his trilby hat on his head and as he opened the conference room door looked back over his shoulder. 'See you Friday, Mr Jacobson.'

Mark stared at the closed door for some moments, then turning to Mr Jacobson he asked, 'So, what do we do now?'

Jacobson gathered his documents and began to return them to the file. 'I knew Benjamin Wise for many many years. There is no possibility whatsoever that he willingly would have signed a document giving anything, let alone his entire estate, to his son Manny.' He paused for a moment, then continued. 'However, that does not rule out the possibility that Manny *has* some kind of document that can contest this will.'

The solicitor's face softened and he smiled at Mark. 'Listen, son, we'll know by three next Friday. In the meantime all we can do is wait.'

Chapter 18

LONDON

THE AER LINGUS FLIGHT EI 111 had touched down in Heathrow airport at exactly 1.05pm. Precisely on time. Throughout the flight and the one and a quarter hour journey by taxi from Heathrow to his apartment on the Edgeware Road, Manny had been very relaxed and confident. When he arrived into the hallway outside his apartment, young Joe Fitzgerald was standing waiting for him.

'What are you doin' here?' Manny asked.

'Waitin' for you.'

'How did you know I'd be home?'

'I didn't, I just knew you'd come home some time!' Joe Fitzgerald spoke softly.

Manny inserted his key into the lock and turned it, the door opened and Joe followed Manny in.

'So, how long are you there, waiting?' Manny asked the junkie as he removed his coat.

'Since last night – I slept sittin' outside the door.'

'Outside my door – all night! You fuckin' asshole,' Manny laughed.

'I need a favour, Manny.'

'Do you now, Joe? And what kind of favour would that be, Joe?'

There was a growing sense inside Manny that the tide was turning against him and he felt agitated. He certainly wasn't in any humour for the Joe Fitzgeralds of this world.

'I need a fix, Manny – bad,' Joe pleaded.

'That's no problem, Joe. Give me the few bob you owe me and the price of the fix and Bob's your uncle!' Manny spoke very flat and matter-of-factly.

'I don't have any money,' the young man mumbled.

'What? Speak up, Joe! What was that? You don't have any money?' Manny's tone was mocking, and the young man just shook his head. 'Well, there's a Russian phrase for that, Joe. Toughski shitski. Now, fuck off, I'm busy.' Manny turned his back on the young man to pour himself a drink.

'*Give me a fix, Manny!*' Joe Fitzgerald screamed as he lunged at Manny Wise.

His decimated form used as much impact as it could on Manny's slumped back. Manny toppled forward, his head going through the glass door of the drinks cabinet, sending bottles of booze and broken glass flying in all directions. But Joe Fitzgerald was undernourished, weak, and disorientated for the want of a heroin fix. He was no match for Manny Wise although the ferocity of his attack had initially caught Manny by surprise. The clash lasted just seconds. After regaining his footing, Manny landed his very first blow, a punch flat to the nose, pushing Joe's cartilage back into his face. The young man dropped to the ground like a sack of potatoes. Even though Joe Fitzgerald was unconscious from the very first blow, Manny continued to kick him for a further thirty seconds or so. Manny was now crazed and his breath was coming in grunts. He walked away from Joe's body and stumbled over a footstool. As he got up from the floor he took with him a bottle of Scotch that had been lying on its side close to his hand. Then he slumped into an armchair and uncorked the bottle.

It was at this precise moment that Derek (Wilco) Wilson, Sergeant Major (retired), rang the police from his apartment below Manny Wise's. In his early eighties and even though still a little scared from his last confrontation with his upstairs neighbour, Sergeant Major Wilson had had enough.

Manny sat pale and shaking, and he gulped hungrily from the bottle. The warm golden liquid burned his throat. He rose from the armchair. Carrying the Scotch he went to the bathroom, and checked the damage in the mirror. There was a three-inch-long gash from his hairline down to the middle of his forehead. It need a stitch. He put the Scotch bottle down on the toilet cistern, deciding to wash the streaks of blood that covered his face. But suddenly changing his mind he decided he would shower later.

He re-armed himself with the bottle and headed for the study. What he really needed now was a snort of cocaine. He wheeled his office chair away from the front of the safe and quickly opened the combination lock. Stretching over the money, he removed the tray at the back. On the top of the tray was a foil-wrapped one-kilo package of cocaine. He picked up the package in his left hand and held it up to his nose, taking a sniff. It was then he thought about the document that had brought him back from Dublin so quickly.

With the cocaine still in his left hand he began to remove the papers in the tray, one by one. Stocks, bonds, a few letters of credit, and then – nothing! The yellowed envelope marked 'Dublin Papers' was not there. He quickly bent to the safe and again with his free right arm began to feel around the back, behind the money. He felt nothing. In a panic he pulled the money from the safe, a couple of bundles burst and the crisp notes scattered across the room like butterflies. Slowly Manny Wise stood erect. He clenched his fingers and raising his arms over his head he slammed his fists into the middle of his desk screaming, 'NO!!!'

Two things happened simultaneously. First, Manny had forgotten that in his left hand he held a foil pack of cocaine, and as his fists hit the desk the bag burst and a huge white gush of cocaine shot towards the ceiling, spreading out like a nuclear cloud. The second thing was a loud bang as the size thirteen black leather shoe of Detective Constable Pete Wilkinson sent the door of Manny's apartment flying wide open. This kick had been delivered with great gusto, for Detective Wilkinson had been waiting over two years to kick down this particular door. The look of surprise on Manny's face as the police poured into his study was matched only by the look of surprise on the officers' faces at the sight that lay before them. Manny Wise had over sixty thousand pounds spread in a circle about his feet. In his left hand he held the remains of what was once a kilo of cocaine. The front of his body and face were completely covered in white dust, except for one three-inch red stripe which ran from his hairline to the centre of his forehead.

In a low voice, Manny said, 'I've been robbed.'

* * *

It was Friday. It was five minutes to three o'clock. Mark Browne sat at his desk in the small office of Senga Soft Furnishings. He was doodling on a workpad. He stopped doodling and rested his head in his left hand and began tapping the pencil on the desk. He stared at the telephone.

In the Tinsely Wire Co. the barbedwire machine ground slowly to a halt. Dermot Browne went to the canteen where he washed his hands and poured himself a glass of milk. He sat down and looked at the canteen clock. The second hand swept slowly around the face. Dermot began to drum his fingers.

Dino Doyle checked the timer on his client's hair-dryer. He reset it by another two minutes. He looked up at the clock. It was three minutes to three. He tossed his comb and scissors into the steriliser unit and made his way to the small room at the back of Wash & Blow hairstylist's. Rory Browne was sitting there at a table with a mug of coffee in front of him, nervously smoking a cigarette.

'Three minutes,' Dino anounced.

'Yeh – three minutes,' Rory replied.

Dino went over to him and gently squeezed his hand. Rory smiled his appreciation.

A couple of doctors returning from their lunch break nodded to the likeable young porter as they passed him. Simon Browne simply nodded back. He had his hands dug deep into the pockets of his porter's coat and he strolled along the corridor at a relaxed pace. When he came to the big brown door he pulled hard on it, for it was quite heavy. He entered, and the door closed slowly behind him. Simon loved the quiet of the hospital chapel. He walked to the nearest pew, knelt and began to pray.

Agnes paid the taxi driver and stepped onto the

pavement to join Cathy. When they went in the door of Senga Soft Furnishings they were met by Betty. The factory was totally quiet.

'What's goin' on here, Betty?' Agnes asked.

'What? Oh the quiet. I don't know, Mrs B, it's been like that since a quarter to three.'

Cathy glanced around the factory. 'Where's Mark?' She asked.

'He's in the office – waitin',' Betty told her.

'I'll go into him,' Agnes began, but Cathy restrained her.

'No, Ma – leave him.'

There was just one telephone in Senga Soft Furnishings. Because the office was sometimes unmanned, Mark had got the Post and Telegraphs people to rig the phone to a large bell that was mounted outside the office. This way, wherever he was, Mark would know when the phone was ringing and could make his way to the office. At two minutes past three o'clock the bell clanged. The staff of Senga Soft Furnishings were well used to this bell going virtually non-stop throughout the day, yet on this occasion it seemed to clang louder than it had ever clanged.

From their vantage point the three women saw Mark standing up as he placed the receiver to his ear. He stood very still. There was little animation. Then they watched as he slowly took the telephone from his ear and replaced it on the receiver. Mark began to walk towards the office door. Agnes glanced over her shoulder and was surprised to see that there were now over forty people standing around her. Wherever they had been just ten seconds before, the phone bell had flushed them out. Mark came out of the office and walked straight across the factory floor to Betty and took her hand. His delivery of the result was very simple.

'It's ours!' He smiled broadly and Betty threw her arms around his neck.

There was a huge cheer from the workforce and a lot of back-slapping and hand-shaking, but eventually everybody drifted back to work.

Mark walked his mother and sister to the corner of the street where he waved down a taxi for them to send them home. While he was organising transport for the two, Betty was standing in the office. On the desk she noticed the pad where Mark had been doodling. It was upside-down and she turned it around to face her. He had drawn an oblong box, inside which he had written just two lines. The top line read 'Mark Browne', the second line 'formerly Wise & Co.'. Betty smiled. She looked through the glass office door to see Mark already organising things and ploughing into the work as if nothing had changed, but she knew better. She turned back to the pad, picked up the pencil Mark had been using, and on the top line of his new sign, beside the name 'Mark Browne' she wrote, 'and Son'.

Epilogue

JUST FIVE DAYS AFTER THE OLD BAILEY sentenced Manny Wise to fourteen years in prison, Joe Fitzgerald died of injuries he had received at the hands of the crazed drug dealer. It had been a long fight for the Metropolitan Police to piece together the evidence that would eventually take down this smug little cockney. During the four months it took the police to put their case together Joe Fitzgerald had remained in a coma. Now for the first time in a long, long time he was finally at peace. His death would result in further charges against Manny Wise, and to the delight of the Metropolitan Police, and for the benefit of the citizens of London, a further twelve years would be added to Manny Wise's sentence.

It was a young police constable walking his beat who accidentally discovered the body of Frankie Browne beneath sheets of newspaper in an alley at the edge of Chelsea, on a freezing November night. The young man's body lay frozen in a foetal position on that minus four-degrees night. An autopsy would later reveal a number of facts. For instance that Frankie had died of hypothermia, that he was a long-time drug abuser, and that he had probably not eaten for at least three days.

Modern technology was amazing more and more people with the secrets it could garner from a frozen corpse. On this occasion however, there was one secret science could not extract. For the last eight years of his short and tragic life, Francis Browne had lived under the name of Ben Daly. Before burning the dead man's ragged clothes, an assistant of the coroner's office went through the pockets in search of anything that might be valuable. They were empty but for a dirty, crumpled envelope upon which was written 'Dublin Papers'.

If you take on one of Agnes Browne's children, you take on them all, wherever they are.